THE COST
of
BETRAYAL

PART II

W.C. HOLLOWAY
"AMERICA'S NEW STORY TELLER"

GOOD 2 GO PUBLISHING

COST OF BETRAYAL: PART II
Written by W.C. Holloway
Cover Design: Davida Baldwin – Odd Ball Designs
Typesetter: Mychea
ISBN: 978-1-947340-47-3
Copyright © 2019 Good2Go Publishing
Published 2019 by Good2Go Publishing
7311 W. Glass Lane • Laveen, AZ 85339
www.good2gopublishing.com
https://twitter.com/good2gobooks
G2G@good2gopublishing.com
www.facebook.com/good2gopublishing
www.instagram.com/good2gopublishing

CHAPTER 1

At 11:00 p.m. in Little Havana, Kitty Cat and her girls made their way to Club Paradise that was owned by Manuel Colon. The night club was packed with family and friends along with regular customers all celebrating Manuel's birthday. Cat got word through the streets about the event. She used her sex appeal and money to find out about Manuel's whereabouts.

Guns were not an option in this place, so they came up with another game plan. The only guns that were permitted in the club were all strapped to Manuel's men.

Cat and her girls blended into the club and danced seductively and alluringly as they all looked around for Manuel based on the description they were given of him. It did not take long to find him, since the birthday boy had chosen to hang out in the VIP lounge that overlooked the dance floor. Cat tapped Mya and Princess and directed their attention above to Manuel.

"There's that punta up there!" Cat said.

"How the hell are we going to get up there past all that security, ma?" Mya asked.

"Magic, watch me work it, niña. He's going to invite us up there!"

They followed behind her over to the bar where she ordered a bottle of Cîroc Blue Dot. She then gave the bartender a message to send up with the bottle.

"This is for the birthday boy. Tell him it's from me. Oh, let him know I said that if he wants to unwrap his gift, me and my girls are down here waiting."

The bartender sent up the bottle with the message as Cat, Mya, and Princess all stood at the bar looking sexy in their tight jeans and tops that pressed against their perky breasts that displayed their tweaked nipples.

Within minutes, the bottle had arrived at his suite. Manuel was surprised when the server delivered the message. He wanted to know where it came from.

"What is that? Who sent it up?" Manuel asked.

"The exotic chic at the bar wearing the tight red jeans."

Manuel stood up and walked over to the balcony. He then looked down to the dance floor. To appear more alluring, Cat had her back turned toward Manuel.

Mya gave Cat the heads-up that he was looking in her direction.

"Cat, that piece of shit is looking down here. He might want you to come up there. He's definitely on it."

"Like I said, mamita, watch me work my magic," Cat said.

She turned a little to expose some of her exotic beauty as she took the cherry out of her piña colada. Cat placed it against her glossy lips in a salacious way before sticking out her tongue to fondle the cherry. She then seductively placed it into her mouth.

Manuel was laughing at the entertainment at the same time his hormones kicked in, when he started thinking with his other head. Without question, just like any other man, he was ready to see more of this exotic beauty and her tricks. So he turned around to one of his goons and told him to immediately bring her up to the suite.

"Mira, go down to the bar and get the sexy chica in the red jeans," Manuel ordered as he pointed toward Cat.

She started to smile, knowing her magic, as she had called it, was working. Now she was one step closer to avenging her baby brother.

Manuel's goon went down to the dance floor, made his way over to the bar, and walked up to Catrina.

"Excuse me, mami, someone would like for you to join them in the VIP suite for a drink."

"Tell that someone only if my girls can come."

"I don't think I want to run back up to the suite

and miss the chance to bring you up, so I say yes to your friends. They can go where you go!"

"Good for you, papi. Now your boss will have the best birthday of his life."

Manuel already had girls in the VIP suite, but when Cat rolled in with her girls, he excused the other females, especially when his mind flashed back to what she had done with the cherry, because he wanted her tongue on him.

"Come over here, mami. Talk to me. I promise I don't bite, unless you like that type of shit. Your friends can make themselves comfortable too. Enjoy the fun!" Manuel said, as he stood by the bar area in the suite.

Cat walked over to him and added sexiness to her salacious walk to lure him in even more as she took each step closer to him.

"Ah, mami, I like what I see. What's your name?"

"Catrina, but my friends call me Cat. That is my girl Mya and my homegirl Princess, right over there."

"Where are you from?"

"Pennsylvania, but we came down here to party and have fun."

Cat did not want to say she was from New York because it could have set off a red flag. She did not want Manuel to be paranoid. She only wanted him to be at ease with her.

Cat flirted with Manuel and tried to make her approach even more convincing. Mya was also doing her thing with José over on the couch in the corner. Cat wanted to put Princess in play so she didn't get left behind, so she whispered into Manuel's ear. Her lips pressed close to him, which only made her words even more sensual.

"Papi, me and my girl can show you a lot of things with our tongues if you like. You can watch her do me. Mmmhh! Just talking about it gets my pussy wet, papi!" Cat said, kissing his ear and then his neck.

Her warm breath sold the moment. Right then, Manuel truly became convinced and wanted her more than anything. He stood up from the bar stool.

"Hey, get the cars ready. We're leaving right now to go back to my house for an after party."

Manuel turned his attention back to Cat.

"I can't wait to see what you and this sexy thigh right here are going to do," he said while caressing her soft ass.

"It'll be our way of saying happy birthday to you, papi," Cat responded.

They all exited the club. Cat and Princess got into Manuel's royal blue Rolls Royce Ghost, while Mya jumped into the black Stealth S600L with José. Both men drove off thinking they were about to score the best sex of their lives. But neither one realized they were sealing their own fates by allowing their dicks to think for them.

CHAPTER 2

Once they arrived back at his mansion, Manuel's security team took their positions around the inside and outside of the property. Mya and José made their way to the guest master suite, while Cat and Princess followed Manuel into his opulent master suite that boasted a California king-size bed, mirrored walls, gold features throughout, a living area, a mini-bar, his-and-her bathrooms, and a massive walk-in closet. Manuel poured each of the ladies double shots of Patrón Silver, and then both of them downed their drinks. But the ladies were there to take care of business, so the alcohol did not affect them at all.

Manuel stood behind Cat and began to kiss her, while at the same time, he pressed his hands against her perky breasts. She let out a light moan to sell it. His hands wandered down to her pants. He then unbuttoned them until his fingers slid into her panties over her landing strip to part her peach. He felt the warmth and wetness of her pussy.

"Ah, like that right there, papi!" she let out.

Princess came around and joined the fun by reaching around and grabbing hold of Manuel's dick. She began to caress it through his pants, making him harder by the second.

"Okay, mami! Let's take the fun over to the bed!" Princess said, turning to undress as she made her way over.

She was fully nude before she crawled into the bed in a seductive manner as she looked back over her shoulder at Manuel with lust in her eyes. He got out of all his clothes and placed his .45 automatic on the nightstand. He was very excited to get this sexual party started with the two women.

Cat revealed her curves of perfection that caught his full attention as her eyes locked with his, which were filled with lust and passion. She then licked her lips as if she wanted him so bad. Truthfully, she just wanted to kill him that bad, so selling this sexual encounter was easy in order to get what she wanted in the end.

"This has to be the best birthday for me ever!" Manuel expressed, trying to take it all in when he saw the two women and their alluring bodies and faces.

"It's all for you, papi! Can you handle it?" Princess asked.

"I'm going to do my best!"

As soon as he lay down on the bed, the two women started allowing their hands and lips to roam over his body. He became engulfed in the seduction and felt on cloud nine, as Princess took his stiff dick and stroked it up and down, which make him harder. She then kissed his dick and balls just to tease him, which made him squirm at her seductive touch. She started to take him into her warm, wet, and slippery mouth, and then continued to stroke him up and down with her soft hand and her lips sucking on him. He felt good and began to breathe in deeply.

"Damn, this is so good, mami!" he let out, when he felt her mouth on him, just as Cat's lips kissed his body and added to his overall sensation of ecstasy.

At the same time, Cat started to move in for his gun on the nightstand, until he pulled her back closer to him.

"Come over here, mami, and get into this. Show me your magic!"

Cat smiled as she went down on his dick, where Princess was already in motion. She stopped only to exchange a passionate kiss with Cat, followed by heavy caressing of each other's breasts, which was something they had already done together in private. Manuel watched the two exotic bitches kiss and touch each other, and he became even more curious and horny as his heart raced just as quickly as his mind did.

"This is some sexy shit right here! I like it, mamitas!"

Cat paused from the kiss and took his dick and kissed around it, before placing it into her mouth. She sucked and slurped it and made him feel so good, until she stopped, only to get on top of him. She mounted him with her wet, warm, and tight pussy, and slowly slid down on him as her tight pussy adjusted to his length and thickness. Right then he felt like he was almost ready to erupt from the intense pleasure of her body accompanied by his excitement and her exotic looks.

"Oh shit, mami! Your pussy truly is like magic. I almost let loose. Mmmm! You feel so good!"

"Ahi, papi. Ahi, ahi!" Cat let out, going all in to make him even more vulnerable, as she worked her hips by going up and down, slamming down on his long, thick dick.

Her vaginal muscles contracted around his member. Cat could see that Princess was trying to move in for the gun, so she started to moan louder and with more intensity.

"Mmmmmm! Mmmmmm! Ahi, ahi, ahi, papi! Ahi, ahi!"

Her words alone triggered his release and made

him bust inside of her. He was unable to hold back any longer.

"Oh my God, mami. I'm cumming!" he shouted, slamming his dick up and into her wet pussy.

"Mmmmm! Mmmmm, papi! Mmmmm, ahi, ahi, ahi!"

Princess looked over at Cat and realized that she, too, was cumming for real by the look on her face. When Cat locked eyes with Princess, she became serious, even in the midst of cumming. She then focused back on the reason they were there.

Princess started kissing Manuel to block the view that she was slipping the .45 over to Cat. As soon as Cat took hold of the gun, her motion of going up and down stopped. Manuel's eyes opened, only to come face to face with his .45 automatic staring back at him. His face could not express more disbelief and shock than at that very moment.

"What's wrong? You don't like my dick or something?"

"Papi, you're stupid! This is about business. The sex was my weapon of choice to get you where I need you. This is for my brother, Young Pablo."

"Wait a minute! Don't shoot me. You don't need to do this. I can give you money or whatever you need!"

"What I need is my brother back, and you took him away from me. So your life is the only thing that will fix it!"

Manuel was a man of power, but now he was caught at his weakest point because he allowed himself to be deceived by their beauty and brains. He looked over at Princess as she was getting dressed. He wanted her to give him an out. Yelling to his men would not do any good.

Princess simply smiled at him before she said, "Happy birthday, papi! But you fucked up bad. Look at it this way, you had the best last birthday any man would die for."

Princess puckered her lips and blew him a kiss of death. At the same time, Cat fired a thunderous round that pushed his brains out the back of his head and into the feather pillow his head had been lying on.

The roar of the gun fire alerted Manuel's men outside the room, so they burst inside. Cat was still on top of Manuel, but she immediately turned around toward the door. She fired off multiple shots and dropped both men with head and body shots. Princess rushed over to the downed men and took their Glock 40s, one for her and one for Mya.

Cat got off of Manuel and wiped herself off with

the sheet before she got dressed. They headed to the guest master suite where Mya and José were in bed. As they entered the room, Carlos Santana was playing loudly on the stereo. José was on top of Mya stroking deep and slow until Princess came up behind him and fired off a couple slugs into his back. The impact knocked him off of Mya. At the same time he felt the hot slugs burn his flesh, he still tried to go for his gun on the nightstand, until Princess ran down on him fast and fired off two more slugs into his face, which canceled all thoughts he had of shooting back.

Cat turned off the music and looked at her girl, Mya.

"Damn, ma, it looks like you was really getting into it with papi."

"It was good dick, plus y'all was taking too long. What else was I supposed to do, push him off of me?"

Mya responded.

"Don't worry, girl, you wasn't the only one having fun!" Princess said as she looked over at Cat.

"That was business, ma, and you know it!" Cat said, breaking a smile.

"Business was feeling good, huh?" Princess joked.

"We have to go. I want to burn this muthafucka down!"

They all raced into the master suite and grabbed bottles of alcohol. They poured the booze onto the bodies and bed, and then set them on fire.

"That's too bad for papi. He fine, too!" Mya said after setting José on fire.

"He's dead now, mami. At least he got some pussy before Princess put him down," Cat said.

As they exited the house, Manuel's goons outside

came around and fired off their weapons, which started a gunfight between them and the ladies. They took out a few goons before taking cover and firing in between ducking down. It got down to one goon left, but he tried to bluff as if there were more.

"Don't make me kill y'all pretty bitches! You can leave now if you want to live!" the Cuban said, taking cover on the other side of the Rolls Royce.

His fumbling attempt to fend them off made them laugh as they closed in on his from each side of the car, until he was faced with three guns staring back at him. He tried to reach quickly and aim his gun. But each of them started to squeeze the trigger on their guns until they were emptied, basically killing him over and over again.

"You should have run, dumbass!" Cat said aloud while looking on at his lifeless body.

She then looked up at the mansion and saw that it was starting to catch fire from within.

"Them dumb Cuban muthafuckas didn't know who they were messing with," Princess announced.

"Revenge is the sweetest thing next to getting pussy, because his dumb ass fell for it. This is for my brother, who I will love always."

"For Chico and Pito, too!" Mya added.

The women all turned and exited as the mansion became engulfed in flames. They left behind a true gang-land massacre.

CHAPTER 3

At 8:15 the next morning, the burnt remains of Manuel Colon and José Rivera, along with other Cuban goons, were found in the mansion and removed from the charred home. The homicide detectives and Miami Fire Department on the scene shared their views to the homicide department on what they believed had started the fire in order to cover up the noticeable bullet-inflicted wounds to the skulls of the deceased.

A roaring engine came from an approaching red Ferrari F450 with a custom white leather interior, white back drop, and chrome rims. The car itself halted the conversation between the homicide detectives and the police department, until they saw that it was a vice cop. Miami Vice's Carlos Rodriguez was a thirty-eight-year-old Colombian-born Latino with a slim build. He was well groomed with dark brown hair that was combed back. He wore a close beard that was shaped up with razor perfection, and manicured nails, and he flowed with gold jewelry and white-framed Ray Ban Aviator shades. He exited his car in a two-piece white linen suit and pants with a red alligator belt that matched his alligator shoes. He looked more like a drug kingpin than a cop.

Carlos made his way over to the homicide detective who was adjusting his shades as he looked on at the damage to the mansion. It was also not hard to miss all the body bags lying on the ground outside.

"Carlos, what brings you over this way? You're a vice cop. Shouldn't you be cracking down on some drug cases at the ports?" Detective Freeman asked.

"Actually, Detective, I came here to help you guys since I know you're having problems solving all the murders that have gone unsolved this year. Anyway, what do you guys have here?"

"This is Manuel Colon's mansion. We have two vics over there who were inside the house. We also have others over there who appear to have been gunned down in a shootout. Casings are everywhere. The fire was set deliberately to cover up the bodies or to make a statement.

"I'm going to take a look around, if you guys don't mind."

"Help yourself, just don't move anything."

Carlos walked over to the first two sets of body bags which the detective had said where of two of the men inside. He squatted down to unzip the first bag and smelled the distinct odor of burnt flesh. He recognized Manuel's body from the length of his frame, the watch, the bracelets, and the chain around his neck, which was now burned into his flesh. Carlos stood to his feet and took out his cell phone to speed-dial an associate in Colombia.

He called Jesus Corales, a six-foot-one vicious killer and right-hand man to Don Renosa. The don was a cartel boss known for his violence and worldwide cocaine distribution.

Jesus was a light-skinned Colombian with short black hair combed back neatly. He had light brown eyes and perfectly tweezed eyebrows.

When Jesus saw the number from America come across his phone, he figured there must be something wrong, because the Colombian cartel had paid a lot of money to assist Manuel in getting his product into the country. He also made sure he got the inside scoop on drug raids and busts.

"You know, when you call, Carlos, things must be wrong, so get straight to it, because I'm very busy."

Carlos was the laid-back type. He was always composed and never needed to raise his voice, because he allowed his presence and power to speak for itself.

"The Cuban and his partner do not look so good right now. They were in a bad fire, but they were dead before the fire, so we have a big problem."

Jesus was at his mansion being catered to by a woman pleasing him orally before and during the call, until he heard about the death of his guy that was moving tons of cocaine for him. He pushed the female's head away from his dick and was now ready to address Carlos on the other end.

"You know what happened the last time I came to America? It was bad for the Russians and the morenos. So what do you think is going to happen now?" Jesus paused and processed his thoughts of the situation, especially thinking about the four tons of coke that he had given to Manuel.

He could not just walk away from this, especially in his position as the number two guy and enforcer for the cartel. Somebody had to pass. Answers were needed, just as the money, drugs, or blood was in exchange for the four tons.

"You're right, Carlos, there is a problem that you better solve. Before my plane lands tomorrow, I want to know who was involved in Manuel's murder and who I am going to kill for our money. If you can't find me anything, then you're dead, too!"

Jesus hung up the phone and left Carlos to take in all that he had just heard. He did not want to die for not finding out what he needed to know before Jesus's arrival. Carlos hopped into his Ferrari and raced over to Manuel's businesses to find out the chain of events the previous day that may have led to his demise. He also called around to people in the hood that were close with Manuel and José. Since he was under a deadline, he had to come up with something in order to stay alive come tomorrow.

Carlos's vice cop instincts kicked in and gave him the idea of checking the cameras at the night club since it was Manuel's birthday last night. Everybody that was anybody in the underground world was there to show love and respect to the drug lord. Depending on the angles of the cameras, they might be able to provide all the information Carlos needed.

He made his way over to the club. The staff members were already on point since he had called ahead. As soon as he entered the club looking all flashy, the employees started cracking jokes on him.

"Hey, Miami Vice is here to arrest everybody!" one female bartender called out.

"I'll arrest all of you if you don't get me what I came for. I need the camera footage from last night, inside and outside."

They gave him what he wanted, and then he headed back to the penthouse by the beach. Carlos got straight to it. He knew that he did not have much time until Jesus would arrive. He needed to get as much information as he could to save himself from being killed, because Jesus would leave him where he stood if he came up short.

CHAPTER 4

At noon the next day back in New York City, Young Pablo's funeral was underway. Cat wanted it to be done quickly to get it over with, and also to make sure that the entire Spanish Harlem neighborhood would come out to show him their love. Even some Latino celebrities that knew of him or knew him came out to show their respect. A few rappers showed up and performed to show their love for the one person who always looked out for them when they were in the game.

Cat, Princess, and Mya all wore T-shirts with Young Pablo's face on them, along with his crew members that were killed. They thought it would keep his legacy alive. It was a true celebration to send off the young kingpin in style.

"Catrina, your brother will certainly be missed and never forgotten. He did a lot for Spanish Harlem."

"Thank you, ma, for coming out to show your love and respect," Cat replied as she leaned in and hugged the lady.

As the young mother walked away, Cat looked on at the crowd of people that came out to show their love.

"My brother will be missed, but he'll always be close to me in my heart."

The celebration event went on for hours until they made it back to Cat's place where she invited over family and friends. She was drinking a Corona and was full of emotions thinking about her brother. She made her way over to the window and stared out at the New York City skyline. She buzzed up thinking about her baby brother and wished he was still there. A lone tear slid down her face as thoughts of her brother when they were kids came to mind.

"Damn, baby bro. We supposed to be at the top together!"

"Excuse me, but I need to see what's up with my girl over there." Mya excused herself from the conversation she was having with one of Cat's relatives and walked over to the window where Cat was standing.

She could see that Cat was a bit distant and not her normal self, and rightfully so with everything that had taken place in her life.

"Cat, you good, ma?"

"Not really. I miss my brother. I wish we had Flaco here right now so I could cut him up one piece at a time so he could feel my pain."

"If you want, we can push through Brooklyn tomorrow looking for his slimy ass."

"He'll get what's coming to him. It's called karma!"

Mya gave Cat a hug to show her love. She knew the pain she was in. They then made their way back over to their guests that were surrounded by liquor, Spanish soul food, and love.

The doorbell rang and got Cat's attention. The first thing that came to mind was that it was the building manager coming to let her know that the music was too loud. Princess made her way to the door to answer it, only to open it and see a badge in her face held by a flashy cop. He was surrounded by a slew of serious-looking Latinos dressed in black two-piece linen suits. It was Carlos who was flashing the badge. He tracked the women down after reviewing the camera footage.

"It's clear who I am. I'm a cop, Miami Vice to be exact. I do recognize your face, but it's your name I do not know. However, I do know you're not Catrina 'Kitty Cat' Alverez. If she's here, then it's perfect, because we all need to talk because we have a problem."

At first, Princess thought they were busted for the work they had put in the previous night. She was going to deny it anyway.

"Why are you here, because you didn't say why or who you really are? Also, why you got all these guys with you?"

Before Carlos was able to speak, Jesus Corales stepped forward with his cigar lit in hand, puffing away at his expensive imported tobacco. He blew the smoke out and filled the air as he walked right past

Princess.

She did not try to stop him because her female instincts kicked in and told her that this muthafucka had absolute power, and that he was not there for small talk or games. Besides, the twenty goons with him followed right behind him one movement. She shut the door behind them as they made their way over to the open living room. Mya and Cat immediately noticed them all walk in, especially Jesus with his shades and still puffing a cigar. Cat grabbed her gun and Mya followed. They were ready to rock out, thinking that shit was about to hit the fan.

Without being told anything, all of Jesus's men removed their weapons with speed and precision and aimed them at Mya and Cat. Jesus turned his head and looked back at his men. He smirked, obviously appreciative of their speed and loyalty. His smile dissipated, however, when he began to talk business.

"I'm sorry about the interruption of your little party, but I believe we have some very important things we need to discuss. I felt a need to come to America personally to see who I'm dealing with, as well as who I'm going to collect almost $20 million from. My associate from Miami tells me that you and your lady friends are the people I need to speak with."

Cat knew what he was hinting at, so she turned and excused her guests, other than her girls. Once they left, she got back to business, hoping that she did not have to bang out with these muthafuckas.

"Now that my guests are gone, what is it we have to talk about?"

"First, ladies, allow me to introduce myself. I'm Jesus Corales. I come from Colombia on behalf of

Don Renosa. You killed Manuel, who was in debt to my boss for four tons of cocaine that he was given. Since it was brought to my attention that you and your lady friends are responsible for his death, my concern now is the money, drugs, or blood. I need to take something back to Colombia."

Cat and her girls had all heard of the powerful Don Renosa on the news. He was blamed for 80 percent of all the cocaine coming into the country.

"That punta killed my brother for money that he thought he didn't have. My brother had the money, but that piece of shit still killed him. As his older sister, I did what I'm supposed to do."

"Like I said, I really don't care about your reasons; it's done. We can't turn back the hands of time. But we can figure out something in order to make this balance of $20 million right."

"Papi, the only money I have right now is right there up against the couch in that bag. There should be close to half a million dollars. I can get more from the streets. Plus, I'm willing to sell my apartment, which is worth $2.5 million."

Cat did not bring up her girls, because it was not their problem. She also wanted to do what she could to prevent a shootout.

"Jesus, we are also willing to do whatever it takes to make ends meet. So if you take this half a mil as a respected gesture, then we can establish a business relationship. I'm quite sure with Manuel gone, someone needs to take his place here in America. We can start here in New York City."

"I respect your willingness to continue on in business. I can tell from the looks of things and by how you ladies handle yourselves, that you can prevail in this business. I'll give you a chance to fill Manuel's shoes. You'll pay your debt back with interest; however, we'll support you with all the cocaine you can move. Trust me when I say, don't ever fuck with our money or we'll wipe out everyone related to you and even those you know—down to the dog. Carlos will get your information and I'll be calling you soon."

Jesus and his men left the high-rise and headed down to the convoy of trucks waiting on them. Carlos had secured their information before leaving.

"Damn, ma, them Colombian niggas is for real about this money shit. I'm glad they gave us a chance to get to this money. We going to be on some boss shit!" Mya said.

"I know, but I just wish my brother was here to see what we've become. Now it's our turn to run

New York City and beyond!" Cat said.

"You already know, ma. I think we should drink to this. Oh that Jesus is smooth and sexy. Mmmmm! But he was about his business for real. I think that is a major turn-on for me," Princess said.

"Get your mind right, Princess. It's time to focus on getting some real money and having real power. Plus, with people like Jesus behind us, Flaco's bitch ass will be easy to get to," Cat suggested after downing her apple Cîroc.

She appreciated her newfound connect and knew that life was about the change for the better.

CHAPTER 5

At 4:00 p.m. the following day in the Bronx, Pauly Fingers was at Goombatas, another one of his restaurants, an authentic Italian place with imported foods from the homeland. He decided to have a sit-down with Cocaine Smitty, who was on his way. The topic was the war between him and the Latinos. It was costing him money and drawing too much attention to the organization. The restaurant was only secured with Pauly's men and staff, and was closed to the public that day. Donte was also going to attend the meeting. While he was waiting, he sipped on a glass of Cîroc Blue Dot.

One of the Mafia goons out front poked his head inside the door to notify Pauly that he had seen

Smitty's car roll around the corner.

"Aye, Pauly, your guy is pulling up out here."

"About friggin' time. This guy would be late to his own funeral!"

Cocaine Smitty exited his Rolls Royce Phantom wearing a dark gray silk suit and black-frame Sean John Aviators. His wrist was studded with diamonds, as were his pinky ring and watch.

He was feeling confident about the meeting, especially now that Young Pablo had been taken out by the Cubans. Also, having the detectives taken care of brought ease to him, because it took off excess pressure and heat. Now he needed to see what was new with Pauly Fingers, since he had told him over the phone that he had good business news that would benefit both of them. Smitty entered the restaurant with his goons and the Italian Mafioso behind him. Pauly and Donte stood up to greet him.

"Smitty, I see you're looking good, just like new money with the silk suit and all. What I gotta do to dress like that?" Pauly asked, messing around.

"You already can afford to look like this, Pauly. I'm trying to catch up to you."

"Aye, Smitty, I like those shades you got there. I need a pair just like that," Donte then chimed in.

"I'll pick you up a pair next time I'm in Sean John's neighborhood."

"Smitty, have a seat. I got some real good Italian food coming out for us."

He sat down ready to enjoy the food, but also to get down to business.

"Smitty, I've been catching a lot of flak with my

family about them dead cops and them Ricans that are way out of control coming into the Bronx where we conduct business. Now I got the Feds sitting on my place over there. I had to friggin' switch cars three times before I came here today. Oh, and this guy Flaco here started this whole thing. But he did come up with a business thing, you know?"

As if it was timed, Flaco came out from the back of the restaurant escorted by Pauly's men. Cocaine Smitty saw this and snapped. He knew that he had been crossed by this muthafucking two-faced bitch-ass nigga.

"What the fuck is going on here? Flaco, you two-faced muthafucka. I knew I should have killed your bitch ass when I first saw you!"

Flaco started smirking at Smitty, which pissed

him off even more. But being a snake himself, he did what he felt was best to survive, because he was a dead man until he came up with some money for Pauly.

Smitty jumped up ready to kill the piece of shit and reached for his gun. At the same time, Donte jumped up with his gun ready in his hand and aimed it at Cocaine Smitty.

"Don't fucking play yourself, Smitty!" Donte voiced firmly. "You might get it off of your waist, but you won't get a chance to pull the trigger!"

"You're turning your back on me, too, like this muthafucka? I showed you nothing but love in this business over the years, and you repay me with this bullshit?"

"The past doesn't pay me. Besides, this isn't

personal. It's a business decision. You know from the years of dealing with me, I never not finish a job that I'm paid to do."

"I'll double whatever you're getting, plus pay you to kill that two-faced muthafucka right there!"

"This thing here cannot be undone, my friend."

Smitty did not even see it coming as the Italian Mafia goons came from behind and killed his men. They dropped them where they stood. Flaco stood back and loved his newfound position of being protected by the Italian Mafia.

"Donte! Pauly! Y'all just going to turn your back on me like this for this two-faced punk?"

"You know, Smitty, I never said that I trusted this spic. I just took his money that he was willing to give up!"

Right then, Pauly swiftly turned and thrust his knife into Flaco's beating heart, piercing it and halting all beats as it ruptured inside of him. He could feel the warmth of his heart spewing inside of his chest. At the same time, his eyes widened in shock of finally being turned on, just as he had done to everyone else. Karma, just like Catrina said, would lead to his end. Pauly turned the knife inside and sealed his fate even more.

"You fucking spic! You can't be trusted! You flipped three friggin' times and started a lot of shit. You deserve this death over and over!" Pauly yelled as he snatched the knife from his flesh and allowed Flaco's body to drop to the floor as he placed the knife back onto the table.

Pauly spit on Flaco's now lifeless body before

shifting his attention back to Smitty.

"Now, back to you. The heat you brought into my life is why our business has come to an end. I can't afford to become a problem to my family. It doesn't turn out well, you know," Pauly said before he tapped Donte on the shoulder as he turned away and added, "Take care of this thing so we can get cleaned up here."

"Fuck you, Pauly!" Smitty yelled out after hearing those words.

He quickly tried to pull out his weapon and get a shot off, but Donte had already gotten the drop on him. He squeezed off two back-to-back rounds that slammed into Smitty's chest and dropped him.

Donte walked around to the other side of the table where Smitty lay barely breathing.

"Fuck you, nigga!"

"Tough guy 'til the end, huh?" Donte said, pumping two rounds into his face, which marred his features and made sure he would have a closed casket.

He then turned toward his uncle, who was walking away.

"Uncle Pauly, the don would like to sever his business ties with you, too."

"Oh no!"

At first, Pauly could not believe what he was hearing, but he immediately knew when he turned around that he was next as he faced down the barrel of his nephew's gun. A bullet raced out of the pistol and smacked him right in the face, crushing the bone structure as it forced its way through his skull and flesh to escape out the other side, ejecting warm flesh, brains, and bones with it.

Donte stood there for a few seconds looking on at his uncle's lifeless body before he tucked his gun into his waistline. He then took a valve of coke and dumped a mini mountain onto this fist. He snorted it and felt the immediate rush of the powdery substance. Then he stood up and dared anyone to say a word about what he had just done.

Don Clericuzio found out through his people that Pauly was responsible for the deaths of the detectives and that he gave Smitty the go-ahead. What made him upset was that when he asked Pauly, he acted as if he knew nothing, so he could no longer be trusted. The don also found out the Feds were watching him. This alone was not good for the family.

All of Pauly's goons stood around waiting on Donte to speak. They wanted to know what was going on, but he first took a moment to allow the rush of cocaine to soar through his brain and body.

"The family had to make changes. It was the big guy's decision. So it is what it is. If someone doesn't like it, just speak up. We're all men here!"

"I think it was a bad decision. The big guy should have at least talked to Pauly, you know?" Pauly's right-hand goomba interjected.

"They did talk. The big guy didn't like the lies he told, just like I don't like what you're saying because it shows that you could turn on this family," Donte responded, swiftly removing his gun and firing on the goon where he stood.

At that moment, he felt both the rush of power

and cocaine all at once.

"I do what I do because it's business. We have to survive out here and separate the weak from the strong. For all I know, this guy could get busted and become an informant one day just because he didn't agree with the way the don runs things. He's done now. So if anyone disagrees with this, say something now so we can deal with it."

He looked around and no one said a thing.

"Now let's get this cleaned up and get outta here!"

CHAPTER 6

Within a few hours, the deaths of a Black Mafia boss, an Italian Mafia capo, and local kingpin, Flaco, were all over the news and spreading throughout the streets of New York City. Cat was at her Manhattan high-rise with her girls. A smile spread across her face and heart when she heard the news. She knew Flaco had gotten what he had coming to him, as did the Black Mafia, which put an end to the long war between them.

"I wish my brother could be here to see this punta get his for all he did," Cat cried.

"Like you said the other day, karma! That shit tracked his ass down," Princess said. "This is our city now, chicas!"

"I'll drink to that! A toast to running the streets," Mya added while holding up a bottle of Corona.

"Hold up, ma! This is to La Primera Damas de Calles," Cat added.

As they toasted to the good life, on the other side of the city, Donte was over at Don Clericuzio's mansion mingling with different Mafiosos of the family. He stepped aside when he received a call from his mother, who wanted to know what had happened to her brother, Pauly, because she too had just seen the news.

"Mom, what's going on over there? You all right?"

"No, I'm not all right. I'm a wreck right now. I just saw the news. What happened to your Uncle Pauly?"

His mother knew the family business and the dangers that came with it. However, she was still torn about the abrupt loss of her big brother.

"Calm down already, Mom. You're gonna give yourself a heart attack!"

"I can't be calm, Donte, until I figure out what happened to my brother."

"Okay, okay, okay! I'ma tell you this. The big guy said it was time and that's it!"

"What do you mean that's it? He's your uncle, ya dumb fuck!"

Donte did not want to keep going back and forth with his mother, especially after the fact that he was about to be made capo of the family for taking out Pauly. So he hung up the phone and left her to her own emotions and thoughts. He then entered the room full of bosses and the don himself. They all embraced him and showed him true Mafia love, as he was about to become one of them: a made man. Donte had taken out Pauly Fingers, one of his family's most feared; and in doing so, he had earned his seat at the table.

"Donte, glad you could make it today. I'm honored to be here and see you become one of us."

"Thanks a lot, Nicky boy!"

"Donte, you came a long way so fast. I remember you when you were just a baby running around the mansion."

"As you can now see, Joey Outlaw, I grew up fast being in this family."

"Donte! Donte!" the don called out, gesturing with his hand as Donte made his way over toward him. "I'm proud of you, Donte. And one day this family will be yours to run. You'll be sitting in this seat. I see a lot of drive in you as well as a promising future. Just keep your mind on the right path!"

"I will, Grandpa. I won't let you down either. I have to keep the family name going."

The don always spoke with patience in his deep-rooted Italian accent, and his words were always received with honor and respect.

"When the day comes, Grandpa, our family legacy will live through me."

"I know it will!" the don replied, giving him a light slap on the cheek.

After the small talk, the sacred induction of La Cosa Nostra began with reciting the words of Omertà. Donte was now feeling the power of being made a Mafia capo. He knew that with this new position, he would have a promising future and a shot at being the don himself one day. He also knew that if the don found out about him snorting cocaine, he would be a dead man. After the ceremony, the other capos and bosses welcomed Donte into their world. Delicious Italian food was served along with stories of the old days. It was a true Mafia celebration.

CHAPTER 7

Six Months Later

Donte was now making a lot of money for the family and himself. At the same time, he left a blood trail in his wake, whacking anybody and everybody that did not pay his money or those he felt were a threat to him and his rise to power. He took it back to the old ways of La Cosa Nostra by shaking down mom-and-pop stores, businesses, and corporations. Nothing was getting done in New York without his permission, where he would get a piece of the money for himself and the family.

Some of the old guys were becoming jealous of how the don praised him for this financial gain and lucrative income. Donte didn't really care too much about the old guys being jealous, just as long as they didn't try anything stupid or interfere with him getting his flow of income to the don, because he would not hesitate to put them down.

Donte took over Paul's Deli and renamed it Paesan's. He also built a crew to work under his command, which included his driver from the Black Mafia; his goomba, Sal Palluzi; and Skinny Pete, who was one of Pauly's guys who had been loyal to the family for a long time.

Mike "Road Dog" Richardson was a loyal driver from the Black Mafia that now ran with him. Road Dog stood six foot six and weighed close to three hundred pounds of solid muscle. The sheer size of his arms alone always drew people's attention. He favored a dark-skinned Suge Knight. He was both street-smart and savvy. The Brooklyn-born associate ran all the cocaine distribution for Donte, and he ran the Black Mafia the way it should have been run— with an iron fist and no bullshit! Donte supplied Road Dog with the cocaine because he did not want to move it himself. He wanted to stay low in that area in case the don found out.

Sal Palluzi was also known as Pretty P, because of the way he dressed. He was always checking himself out in the mirror. Even when he was whacking a guy, he was more concerned about looking good. He stood five foot ten and had a medium build. He was clean-shaven with black hair and blue eyes, and he had a strong New York accent. Pretty P loved the women and gambling, but he definitely was a true wise guy when it came to taking care of business.

Skinny Pete was the oldest of the crew at fifty-five years old. He stood six foot two and was slim. He was also clean-shaven and had brown hair with a little gray that displayed his years of wisdom, as he would say. Skinny Pete was the hit man you never saw coming. He once whacked a guy in the confessional booth at the Catholic church because he refused to pay the family his debt. The crazy thing is that this guy confessed all of his sins, not knowing that Skinny Pete was on the other side holding the priest at gunpoint to keep him quiet. That was in the old days.

Today, Skinny Pete and the rest of the crew were all a force to be reckoned with, especially being at the top of their game feeling themselves, their success, and their positions of power. They were all eating at Paesan's while laughing and talking about business.

"Aye, Sal, next time we go do a job, I'm bringing you a freaking mirror," Donte said while sipping his fruit punch. "Aye, listen here, we're trying to put this cunt in the truck. He was a little dirty, you know, in case he tried to get away, until I fired one in his ass. Anyway, I'm stuffing this piece in the trunk. Pretty P here is wiping himself off, and then he whips out a comb and starts running it through his hair like some broads are coming," he said as his entire crew started to laugh. "Oh, oh, that's not it. After I get the guy in the trunk, we get in the car and Sal turns to me and says, 'We got 'im, huh?' I said, 'Jesus Christ, we? You didn't do anything but comb your freaking hair the entire time!'"

The crew laughed knowing how Pretty P was.

"Aye, Donte, I put a bullet in his head. Don't forget to mention that, ya know!"

"Okay, I'll give ya that much!" Donte replied, taking a bite of his provolone and pastrami sandwich.

"Skinny Pete, give us some of your stories from the old days," Road Dog said.

"Maybe some other time. I don't want to bore you guys with my old stories."

"Now, Pete, we wouldn't be here if it wasn't for guys like you, the real gangsters who made La Cosa Nostra possible."

Skinny Pete gave a brief smile and accepted the compliment. He took a few gulps of his cola before reflecting back to his old days.

"All right, I went to do this job in a small town in Pennsylvania called Mechanicsburg. This guy I'm after was a rat who was relocated with the Witness Protection Program, but you know we have our sources to find out things. Anyway, I get to this guy's house and it was dark in the spring time. I snuck into the window to get this guy, but for some reason, he must have heard me coming, because when I got into the bedroom, I heard the front door slam. So I looked out the window and he was hauling ass." The crew began to smile at his story. Pretty P was already laughing, just thinking about the guy running.

"So this guy's running and I started down the steps and through the door. I knew I couldn't let him get away, because the Feds would really put him in hiding. I got into the street and ran after him. Now remember, I was a little in shape back then with the cardio thing. So I was on his tail with my .22 caliber revolver. We ran for a few blocks and in mid-stride he turned his head around and yelled out: 'Aren't you tired of chasing me?'" Dante and the crew burst into laughter. Sal almost choked on his drink.

"So did you catch him, Skinny Pete?" Road Dog asked.

"Yeah, hold on, let me finish! So this guy's running, and I didn't want to shoot him while running in a quiet neighborhood, but a cop car was coming our direction and he ran into the street. The cop didn't even see him, so he gets smacked by the police car. Now the cop gets out and I go up to see if this guy's dead. As soon as he sees my face standing over him, he started pointing at me, so I pumped two into the cop's head and the other three into this guy's face, and I left him like that!"

"That's some real old-school gangster shit right there," Road Dog said.

"La Cosa Nostra. Nothing comes in between it!" Donte said.

Pretty P was sipping his drink. He was ready to add to the conversation until Donte's cell phone sounded off. When he looked down at the number, it was another capo, Joey Outlaw, down in Miami. He pointed to his phone that read: Joey Outlaw.

Skinny Pete's eyebrows raised. He wondered why Joey was reaching out to Donte, especially since he was not everyone's favorite since he outshined them all. Donte tapped the screen and answered the call to see what he had to say.

"Hey Joey, what did I do to deserve the honor of this call?"

"Business, kid. It's always business, never forget! Anyway, I got this guy down here, and he's looking to move around up there. I figured I'd give you a call on this. He's into a lot of things I don't want to broadcast over the airwaves. He goes by Bobby V. He brings it in down here. I figured I'd give you guys a heads-up and you can go from there."

"So this guy you're wanting me to invite into my circle, he's good? You vouch for him?"

"Of course, I wouldn't be dealing with him if he wasn't."

"So how long have you been dealing with him?

"About five months ago we linked up."

"Joey, you know I run a tight circle up here, plus we got a good thing going with me and the guys." Donte paused before he gestured for Skinny Pete to see what he thought. Skinny Pete nodded his head for the go-ahead. "Okay, Joey, tell your guy to meet me here tomorrow. Aye, he better be who you says he is."

"Hey, kid, I've been doing this thing here before you were born, so don't ever question my judgment!" Joey Outlaw said before hanging up.

"Skinny Pete, what do you think about Joey's guy? You've been around Joey long enough to know if he's up to something."

"Let's see what this new guy looks like and his story. If he's a cop or inside man for Joey trying to see what we're doing up here, we'll kill him either way."

"He better not be either of those things, or I'll cut his balls off and stuff them in his mouth."

"I'll have a check on this guy before he gets here just to play it safe," Sal said.

"Good thinking, Sal. If anything looks out of place, I want to know about it before this guy gets here," Donte anxiously said, and looked forward to meeting the new guy.

If he was a money-maker, it would mean good things for his crew and more smiles from the don when he arrived with more money. If not, then Joey Outlaw would have to watch his back.

CHAPTER 8

Kitty Cat, Mya, and Princess were in Bogatá, Colombia, just getting off of Jesus's private G4 jet, along with Carlos, the vice cop. Don Renosa wanted to meet the women that were moving his product with ease. He also wanted to put a face with his customers.

It was Cat and her girls' first time in the country, as well as the first time they had the chance to meet the notorious drug lord, so they were a little nervous but still looked sexy at the same time. Cat had her hair pulled back, and she wore light makeup. She had gloss on her lips, and her eyes were outlined to make them really stand out. The YSL jeans fit tight and flowed with her white T-shirt that exposed her flat stomach and naval ring, which was just one of the many piercings she had.

Mya's long hair rested over her powder-blue light cotton Prada sweat suit that flowed with her Nike Air Jordan IIIs. Her ass looked soft and pressed up against the sweat suit. From behind, her ass bounced as she stepped off the jet.

Princess also wore her hair pulled back with her tail braided and lying over her shoulders. She looked stunning with her radiant red lipstick that matched her white sports top with red lettering in glitter that read: "I am the baddest bitch!" The shirt represented her true identity on the streets yet flowed down to her flat stomach and curves that flowed over red Gucci jeans that hugged her ass and thighs.

Outside the jet were four G55 Mercedes Benz trucks waiting with security in the first two trucks. The other two trucks were for Carlos, Jesus, and the ladies, and were all provided by Don Renosa. Cat and Princess got into the truck with Jesus, while Mya followed Carlos to the last truck. They all knew by the way this convoy had come to pick them up, that shit was serious with meeting the man behind it all. He made certain that they arrived without any problems.

"So this is the place that makes it all happen?" Mya said.

Carlos simply smiled, since he knew what she was implying.

"This country is also known for its beauty. Most people don't take the time to appreciate it all."

"It is a beautiful place. I would like to see more of it."

"In time, Mya. I'll show you this country's best-kept secrets and beautiful landscapes."

Carlos found all of the ladies to be attractive, but Mya stood out to him.

The convoy of trucks headed toward the one thousand-plus-acre compound where Don Renosa resided with hundreds of guards around the clock protecting him and his empire. The compound's main house was twenty thousand square feet and had indoor and outdoor pools, a spa, gym, theater, two guest villas, tennis courts, basketball courts, golf course, and other amenities that allowed him to enjoy and entertain guests, including horses, a gun range, go carts, and more.

As the convoy pulled into the compound, the ladies saw the many armed guards spread out with AK-47s. Jesus and Carlos helped the women out of the trucks and stood by waiting on Don Renosa. His soldiers came up to the women and searched them.

"It's business, ladies. He has to protect himself, which is his best asset," Jesus said upon seeing the look on Princess's face.

Once the soldiers were done with the search, they called the boss and made him aware of his guests being present.

Within minutes, he came out accompanied by six soldiers, three on each side. He also carried his gold-plated .45 Desert Eagle that was exposed in the waistline of his cream-colored Armani pants that flowed with his aqua blue silk shirt that matched his alligator sandals, giving him the ultimate look and comfort. The necklace he wore had two carat diamonds around it with a military tag that read El Jefe at the top and Droga, Dinero, Y Sangre at the bottom.

The light-skinned Colombian boss stood six foot

one and had a medium build. He was well groomed and manicured, with black hair cut close and combed back, close beard shaped up, and thick eyebrows that he took his thumb across as he approached the women and saw how beautiful they were in the flesh. He thought they were even more beautiful than Jesus had described them. As he walked up to them, the women did not how to react since he looked so serious.

"Ladies, you are beautiful, driven by money, and yet deadly. This is one helluva combination. I'm glad to finally meet the three of you. Jesus speaks only good things about you all. He says that you're moving five tons a month in New York. As for the thing with Manuel, you handled it well, especially picking up where he left off and moving more product and becoming a stronger force with the three of you."

"Don Renosa, it's even more of a pleasure to meet you. Me and my girls have heard things about you in the media; but to come face-to-face, I feel like we're finally getting somewhere as females in this game," Catrina said.

Don Renosa appreciated how she spoke, as well as how her team carried themselves looking good but being professional.

"Ladies, let's go inside my house instead of standing out here. We can finish talking in the air conditioning. If you ladies are hungry or would like a drink, just let me know and I'll have my staff bring whatever you desire," he offered before leading the way back to the mansion with his soldiers following alongside of him.

Once inside, everyone requested and received

their drinks.

"I could get used to this type of living and service," Cat said while drinking her apple martini.

Don Renosa reached forward and took a few grapes off of the silver tray that also carried cherries, strawberries, and other fresh fruit.

"There is no other way to live. I have worldwide distribution, so money comes in and allows me to be in this position. However, I come from nothing, so I appreciate all that I have. No one can or will take this from me."

Cat was definitely attracted to the boss's power and lifestyle.

"I take it the lady of this big house loves the spoiled lifestyle you give her?" she said with a smile, sending her words with ease.

"Catrina, I like your approach. It's intriguing yet

direct. I'm very single, because I've been unable to find the one to give balance to this life I live."

"So it's true. Being at the top does get lonely!" Cat asked with luring eyes.

She wanted to know more about him, and she wanted to get closer not just physically but also emotionally.

"Mmm, mmm, niña. Y'all two would look good together," Princess whispered lowly to Cat.

Don Renosa was just about to tell Cat that he would like to speak with her without her company to see the personal side of her since he already knew the business side of her. She was a reflection of him. That is what he saw in her thus far, but he could not express that thought now. He was then interrupted by one of his soldiers that walked into the room and over to the couch, leaned over, and whispered into his ear.

Whatever the goon had to say, it was bad, because his body language and facial expressions had changed. He grabbed a few more grapes from the tray and then stood up.

"Ladies! Jesus! Carlos! Would you all please walk with me. I want to show you ladies how I stay in power."

"They all followed him as he walked out into the compound accompanied by his soldiers. They made their way over to the horse stables.

They did not go inside the stables because the person they came to see was already outside secured between two horses. He had one arm and leg tied with ropes secured to the horse on the left and his other arm and leg stretched out to the horse on the right.

"Geramy Lucas, you're the piece of shit attorney

general in America that seems to have it out for me. You want me to be extradited to the States for prosecution. You're even trying to get the government to help you bring me down. I can't allow that to happen," Don Renosa said in an angry yet calm tone.

Carlos, Mya, Princess, and Cat looked on at how helpless Geramy looked. But this was how they got shit done in Colombia. They also realized that this was a feat that could only occur here and not in the States.

The Attorney General was scared, but his words did not show it.

"You're all going to jail! All of you goddamned Spics! You think you can flood our country with drugs and pollute our streets and poison our kids!"

Don Renosa pulled out his Desert Eagle and

quickly aimed it at Geramy. He fired a thunderous round into his shoulder that almost severed it from his body.

"Aaaggghh! You motherfucker! You're still going down, and you won't even see it coming!"

Cat came to Don Renosa's side. She wanted to display her ruthless abilities.

"Papi, let me see your pistol. I'll show him pain!"

"Catrina, no one touches this one. Hey, give me your pistol," he demanded one of his soldiers give up their sidearm, a 9mm automatic that he handed to Cat. "Show me how you work. Impress me!"

She turned with the pistol in her grip as she approached the AG, ready to show him what pain really was. She also wanted to show off her skills and allow Don Renosa to see that she was more than a pretty face.

"Señor Lucas, do you have any kids?"

"Yes, I have kids. What the fuck do you care?"

"I don't care. This means you won't be needing these, punta!" Cat said after she pressed the 9 mm against his left ball and fired off a round, which knocked the wind out of him.

The shot sent an excruciating pain through his body, which made him unable to let out words as he tried to embrace the intense pain. At the sight of this, Jesus, Don Renosa, and Carlos all squinted their faces as they cupped their own balls, knowing had badly it had to hurt.

Geramy bled profusely and was in unbearable pain.

"Now, señor Lucas, you mentioned that Don Renosa was going down and he wouldn't see it coming. So who is this inside person?" she questioned as she placed the 9 mm against his other testicle, which made him breathe heavily in fear of being shot again.

"Miami! Miami. Now kill me, you crazy bitch!" he pleaded, wanting to escape the pain he was feeling that seemed to be draining the life and will to live from him.

Don Renosa appreciated Cat's angle to get the information needed, because he would have just killed him.

"FBI! Vice! Someone you wouldn't expect. Kill me! Kill me! You dumb Spic!"

At the sound of "vice, Miami, and the FBI," Don Renosa shifted his .45 Desert Eagle toward Carlos's face.

"You're with Miami Vice. Who and what the fuck is he talking about?"

Carlos was shocked at this sudden shift with a gun being aimed at him.

"Don Renosa, I swear it's not me he's talking about. I've been loyal to you from day one. There are two new vice cops that came on two weeks ago. Maybe he's talking about one of them."

He then turned to Cat, who was already in position to get information from the AG.

"Mr. Lucas, have you ever seen this man before?" Don Renosa asked, pointing the gun at Carlos.

Geramy smirked through his pain. He knew he would never figure it out until it was too late.

"No, someone closer, and you can't stop it. It's already too late, you dumb Spic!"

Don Renosa did not like what he was saying or how he was saying it. Besides, his lack of information at this point was pissing him off.

"Oye, let the horses tear this punta in half!"

"No! No! Nooooo!" he yelled out as the horse whip cracked and forced the horses to run in opposite directions, pulling him apart while he was still alive. His limbs and torso twitched from the shock, and he let out, "It's too late!"

The attorney general died as the blood poured out of his body where his limbs once were.

"Carlos, when you get back to the States, I want you to find out what this piece of shit knew. No excuses. Find out everything!"

"Yes, boss, I'll get on that as soon as possible," he responded nervously.

Cat handed the gun back to his soldier and then walked over to Don Renosa as he continued to speak to everyone on what was needed.

"Jesus, I want you to use the resources we have to find out who the attorney general is talking about. Then let me know, so we can wipe them and their family out."

"Okay, boss. Ladies, it's time to head back to America."

"Everybody except for Catrina. I want to show you my appreciation for what you've done here today. Because of you, I know more about this inside scum in my organization."

Cat looked at him silently and accepted his proposal to stay. She secretly loved the idea of being with this man who had absolute power. It turned her on by the second just thinking about it.

Cat hugged the girls as they exchanged their goodbyes.

"Hey, ma, don't do anything I wouldn't do!"

Princess joked.

"You tripping, ma. I'ma do everything you would do, and maybe some extra shit!" Cat replied, which made her girls laugh.

"Don't give all the goodies away, ma!" Mya said, tapping Cat on her ass.

As she was saying her goodbyes to her girls and hugging them, Don Renosa was on his phone calling into the house to make reservations for the evening, night, and next morning. With the five-star service of a resort, he had everything he desired right there.

"Make sure y'all hold the business down until I get back."

They all left and headed back to the convoy of trucks that had brought them there. Carlos was thinking about who was close to their organization that could bring them down. The girls were thinking about what had just happened, but more importantly the future of business with Don Renosa.

"Catrina, now I can give you the official tour and even cater to your every desire while you're here as my guest."

"I look forward to being treated like a queen," she said with a smile after taking his hand as he led the way to begin the tour that would allow them to talk on a more personal and intimate level.

CHAPTER 9

A few hours had passed by, and Don Renosa was still showing Cat the other side of him. She loved the treatment from the staff and Don Renosa himself. They ate, talked, and laughed as they made their way up to the master bedroom suite that was larger than most presidential hotel suites. It boasted two fireplaces, mostly for decoration, that added to the opulence of the room. One fireplace was inside the large his-and-her bathroom, while the other was off to the side of the California-king-sized bed. The room also boasted a large Jacuzzi less than twenty feet from the bed, directly off the lounge area. The flowing features of the room were gold, cream, and silver.

As they entered the bedroom, Don Renosa pointed over to the plush chair on the other side of the bed that was close to the large bathroom. In the chair he had lingerie his staff purchased for Cat.

"This is a little something to make you feel comfortable tonight. When you wake up in the morning, these clothes are for you as well."

"How do you know my sizes?" she asked with a smile, yet impressed.

"Not only do I pay attention to details, but I pay my staff enough money to pay attention as well. One of the ladies saw you and took measurements. If they don't fit, then she's fired."

Cat was speechless as she embraced his suave approach to her and how it was a completely different side of him that no one else would ever see.

"I take it the smile on your face is your way of

thanking me?"

"Yes! Yes, thank you for doing this. Now let me go slip into this lingerie so you can see how your gift looks on me," she said while walking into the bathroom.

As she headed toward the bathroom, she noticed the rose petals around the Jacuzzi with red and gold candles surrounding it, which set the mood and allowed her to see the romantic side of him.

It did not take long before she exited the bathroom and looked sexy, with her hair flowing over the cream-colored silk kimono that covered her red lace negligee that pressed against her fit body. Her nipples kissed the fabric and appeared to want to be exposed and be seen. She saw that he was already in the Jacuzzi, so she made her way over to him standing on the side. This allowed him to take in all her beauty and see that the gift he had gotten her was worth every dime. She let the silk robe slide off her shoulders and down over her flesh until it hit the floor. It revealed the best part: the red lace negligee. His eyes took in the true art of her beauty, and he appreciated every moment of it.

"Unbelievable. You look amazing, and even more than I expected. Where have you been hiding, Catrina?"

She lit up inside and out from having someone appreciate her beauty and presence. She leaned down and kissed him. He cherished the feeling of her soft lips as the moment ignited with passion.

"I'm here now, papi! If you like what you see and how I make you feel, then I'll stick around!" she responded as she slid her hand across his chest and down under the bubbles of the Jacuzzi to reach his manhood. He loved her touch as well as her lips close to his ear, as she sensually whispered, "I want you inside of me, papi!"

She stood up and slid out of her lingerie and then stepped into the Jacuzzi looking like she was at a photo shoot. He pulled her close to him and placed his lips on hers. She then wrapped her legs around him and mounted him under the water, sliding down on all of his length and thickness and making her body feel good. At the same time, he was also stimulated by her warm and tight pussy. Heavy breathing and moaning filled the air as he squeezed her ass and assisted her up and down movement on his dick.

"Mmmmm, mmmmm, ahi, ahi! Ahi, papi. Mmmmm!"

Her moans against his ear made him feel good

and stimulated his movements. Each stroke felt better than the last, making their orgasmic sensations stir in their bodies as they built up with each stroke up and down, side to side, deeper and harder. She could not hold back as the sensation raced through her body. She had butterflies in her belly.

"Ahi, ahi, ahi, papi! Mmmm! Mmmm! I'm cumming! Ahi, ahi! Mmmmm!"

She let out a surge of feelings and sensations that stormed through her body and made her pussy pulsate. She wanted to go harder up and down on his dick and feel all of him. She could not hold back any more as she reached her orgasmic peak and came over and over as her pussy squeezed on his dick.

"Ohhh, papi! Mmmmm, oooohhh! It feels so good, papi!"

Her lips were still against his ear. The intimate

sounds made it harder as his soldiers were racing through his body into hers, flowing deep with each stroke. With his hands squeezing her ass as he stroked harder and deeper, it made her cum even more. She felt the wave of pleasure take over her body.

"Ahi, ahi, ahi, ahi, papi! Mmmmmm, mmmmm, mmmmm! Ahi, ahi, ahi!"

They were both cumming at the same time and sharing this intimate wave of orgasmic sensation that soared through their bodies and allowed them to connect physically and emotionally. Her lips came around to his, kissing him with passion as her hips moved and gyrated on his dick. Her orgasm continued at the same time, which made her pussy squeeze his dick and get all of his flow inside of her.

"Your dick is making my pussy feel good, papi!"

she said while looking into his eyes and still gyrating her hips.

He was without words, but he loved the way her pussy felt to him. He also appreciated the look in her eyes and the notion of having a beautiful woman want him as much as he wanted her in every way.

A man with his power did not like to feel weak or vulnerable, but in this very moment he shared with her, it was worth the feelings he had of wanting her to be with him in more ways than this. They would be the world's most notorious and powerful couple, something he thought about as they continued being intimate throughout the night. As they made their way to the shower and back to the bed afterward, they fell asleep in each other's warm and intimate embrace.

CHAPTER 10

Around nine the following morning, Don Renosa was awakened by one of his staff buzzing on the intercom at the side of the bed.

"Good morning!"

"Good morning, señor Renosa. This is Melania calling to let you know that breakfast for you and your guest is ready and at your door."

"Give me a few minutes, and I'll let them in."

"Si, señor!"

He had forgotten all about the breakfast and the time he had told them to come. He then glanced over at Cat, who was still sleeping yet looking sexy even while resting. He almost did not want to wake her up. He would rather appreciate her sleeping beauty.

"Hey, mami! Get up! It's time to eat breakfast."

Cat opened her eyes and scanned the room, and realized that the night before was real.

"Mmmmm, so last night wasn't a dream?"

"No, beautiful. We really enjoyed one another's time, touch, and treasures," he said while getting out of bed and making his way over to the door and opening it. "Come on in, and set the food up over there."

"Si, señor. Is there anything else you would like this morning?"

"This is all for now!"

Cat loved this catered lifestyle, since it felt like she was on vacation, but this was his everyday life of five-star treatment. She sat up and smelled the cheese eggs, steak, bacon, home fries with onions, toast, and grape juice on the side. He turned on the large 65-inch wide screen to watch the news. A picture of Attorney General Lucas came up as a reporter was speaking. Don Renosa turned up the volume to listen.

"US attorney general Geramy Lucas, who's been leading the investigation into the notorious Don Renosa of Colombia, has been missing for over twenty-four hours now. As we're told, it is abnormal for him not to have come home, since he's a family man that would never walk out on his loved ones. His wife reported him missing to the police and made them aware that something had happened that was very wrong. Federal authorities will be looking into this active case that will soon be over as we're told. I'm Christopher Mills here at CNN. We'll bring you more of this story as it unfolds."

Don Renosa changed the channel as he voiced his thoughts on what was just said.

"These fucking people want to bring me down. They think they can take me away from all of this!"

"Chill, papi. You're not going anywhere, especially if I can prevent it. I'm here for you, and when I go back to the States, I'll help you find out who the mole is."

"I have to find out fast before it gets out of control. I want whoever it is to pay. I want their family to pay!"

Cat started to caress his shoulders because she wanted him to calm down. Her touch put him at ease.

"Together, we'll make him pay. I'll ride for you no matter what."

He was feeling the way she was talking. She

could easily be the balance to his life that he was looking for.

An hour later and they were outside of the mansion standing by the Range Rover Sport that was preparing to take Cat to the airport, where his private jet would fly her back to America. He pulled out a suede jewelry box and handed it her. When she opened it and saw the two-carat diamond bracelet, she lit up and smiled inside and out.

"You know how to make a lady smile. Thank you, papi. It's beautiful."

"You're welcome. But know this diamond is not nearly as beautiful as you are. This is my way of showing you how much I appreciate your presence here. I want you to know that you're welcome back any time, so just call and I'll send for you."

"Give me a hot kiss, papi!" she said, coming in close to get a kiss and a hug, which actually made her feel even more appreciated.

The kiss was long and very intimate, as if it was the last time they would see one another. Maybe it was the distance that made them enjoy the moment.

"Take care of yourself, papi. I'll see you soon."

"I look forward to it," he replied as he watched her walk away.

He took in all her beauty, front and back, as she got into the truck. She then waved as it pulled off and took her to the airport. She rolled down the window and leaned her head back. She could only smile when she thought about the night before and the new life she could have each time she visited him. Life and business could not be any better.

CHAPTER 11

At 10:15 a.m. at FBI Headquarters in Miami, agents were gathering around in preparation to listen to the lead investigator. Agent Davis, an Atlanta-born African-American knew the streets, especially working undercover on many cases to rid the streets of drugs. Now his focus was on taking down Don Renosa to make a statement to the cartels about their product finding its way into the US.

Agent Davis stood six foot four and weighed 260 pounds of muscle from hitting the gym daily, which showed in his massive arms. His bald head added to his manly muscular looks. When he entered the room and stood in front of others who were undercover, his presence made all their loud chatter quieten to silence.

"Good morning, sir. Glad to see you."

"Good morning. It sounds like a bunch of shit to me, Agent Perez. I'm not having a good morning, and this is not just directed at you. We have a missing attorney general, who we can already assume is dead. I know we need to bring this case to a close. Now, Agent Perez, tell me what you have on this case."

Agent Perez stood dressed in civilian clothing and looked the part of a queenpin.

"Sir, what I can tell you is the AG is dead. I witnessed this with my own eyes. He suffered a great deal being shot in his testicles, and then two horses pulled his limbs apart."

"Damn! That shit had to be painful, especially with the horses."

"What's painful, gentlemen, is that we can't tell his wife that he's dead or how he died until this case is closed, because it will compromise our case and agents in the field," Agent Davis added.

"Sir, Catrina 'Kitty Cat' Alverez assisted in this. It was her way of showing off for Don Renosa. He fell for it because she stayed behind with him. Mr. Lucas did mention how close we are to taking him down and about the bureau here in Miami."

"Agent Perez, good work. Now, we have to wait on the Colombian government to cooperate."

"He has a small army surrounding his compound at all times, so it won't be easy."

"Nothing in life is easy. That's all for now, ladies and gentlemen. Stay in character. Everyone is excused except for you, Mya. We need to talk."

Mya Perez was an FBI undercover agent. She was also Cat's good friend since childhood; however, when she was twelve, her father took a job in Virginia that separated them until a few years ago when she came to investigate her friend's brother, Young Pablo. In the process, she discovered that her onetime childhood friend was also deep into the heroin game, so she took on another role going deep in cover, including having to sleep with men she would never give the time of day to outside of this role she was playing. She even had to pull the trigger a few times to convince those around her of her loyalty. After Young Pablo was killed, Don Renosa came into play, so she figured she could have a big part in taking down one of the world's most notable drug lords since El Chapo.

Mya walked up to her boss and wanted to know what he had to say.

"I'm worried about you being so deep undercover for as long as you have been. You know if you make the wrong move or decision while under, this could go really wrong, especially dealing with people of Cat's and Don Renosa's stature."

"I'm good, sir. They'll never expect me; besides, we were friends as kids, remember? Also, the vice cop, Carlos Rodriguez, check into him. He's as crooked as hell and working for Don Renosa. He has something arranged that allows the cocaine to get into the country. Another thing, Attorney General Lucas recognized me. When asked if Carlos was the inside man, he looked at me and smirked. But he stayed strong until the end, even when he was being tortured."

"Like I said, this is a dangerous situation you're in. I can pull you out if you want."

"Leave me in. If you take me out now, there will be red flags. How's my son?"

"He misses his mother, so take care of what you have to do and get back."

Mya's three-year-old son, Travon, was the love of her life; however, being deep undercover she had only seen him a few times, which had been hard for her.

"Well, let me get out of here before I get emotional thinking about my son and lose focus on the job. I will need a long vacation after this, just me and my son."

"You earned it, Agent Perez. You surely deserve it," he responded as she walked out and headed back to New York to link up with her crew.

CHAPTER 12

At 12:14 p.m., Donte and his crew sat in the back of Paesan's at the round table and prepared to conduct business with Bobby V. He was a forty-two-year-old, five-foot-ten, 190-pound hustla. Bobby was glowing with his Miami tan and trimmed-up eyebrows, which he always ran his thumbs across as he talked fast trying to hustle someone. He definitely had a knack for pushing product off on people with his fast-paced swagger.

"So, Bobby V, I hear from my associates that you're trying to move north with your business. So what's this move about? Miami not good to ya?" Donte asked.

Skinny Pete, Road Dog, and Pretty P were also

present, and they made sure Bobby V was what Joey Outlaw said he was.

"I'm into expanding like any good businessman, you know?" Bobby V said before going into sales mode and speaking fast to convince his customers. "Okay, okay, I do exotic cars and exports. You know, like Ferraris, Lambos, Maybachs, Vipers, SLR McLarens. You name it, and I got or I'll get it. I got Asians that pay good money for this shit. Plus, I got diamonds: blue, yellow, white, and black chocolate. Any cut, you name it. Take a look here."

He pulled out a black velour cloth pouch that contained loose diamonds. The crew all leaned forward as he opened the bag and laid them out on the table for them to see.

Donte picked one up and inspected it visually.

"I see you have good quality jewels here, Bobby V. But my question to you still remains unanswered. How do I benefit from this?"

"Yeah, yeah, okay. I also move a little of the white stuff. You know, I even toot a little here and there, but it doesn't stop me from doing my thing, you know. Okay, anyway, you come into play by getting me customers, and then you get a cut of my performance since this is your city. Just like I do for Joey Outlaw down there."

"I want 50 percent on anything you do in my city!"

"Jesus Christ! What is this? I can't eat off of 50 percent being given away. I give Joey 20 percent, which is good considering he's not doing anything."

Donte fondled the diamond in his fingertips and

listened to Bobby V talk him down, while trying to pierce through him to see what he was really about.

"I'm not Joey Outlaw, as you can see. The lowest I'll go is 30 percent, and it's non-negotiable."

The room fell silent as the crew sat looking on at Bobby V and awaiting his response.

"Okay, okay. You're busting me up here, but I can do 30 percent. Now what about the other thing?"

"What other thing?" Donte responded. He knew exactly what he meant, but he wanted to keep the door closed on that business since he could not trust most people.

"You know, the white stuff. The cocaine! I'm trying to make a living here and have fun on the side."

As the old guy of the crew, Skinny Pete stood

from his chair. He had a gut feeling that something was now wrong with this guy. He came up behind him and massaged his shoulders and felt his tension.

"Bobby V, how long have you known Joey Outlaw?" Skinny Pete asked, searching for answers to corner the guy.

Bobby V was nervous when he saw the seriousness on everyone's faces. His heart began to pound and his mind raced as he tried to find the right words.

"I met Joey about a year and a half ago over at the Miami ports. He saw me and my guys loading cars and became curious, and we started from there."

As always, Donte had his weapon at the ready. This time it was a 10 mm Taurus loaded with one in the chamber that was ready to go.

"Bobby V, Joey said you guys recently met a few months back, so a year and a half ago doesn't match up."

"Did I say a year? I could have gotten him confused with other business deals I have going on, you know?"

Skinny Pete grabbed Bobby V around the neck as Donte brought his gun into view. Pretty P stood up fast and checked Bobby V by tearing open his shirt.

"You better not be wearing a wire!" Pretty P yelled. "No wires here, but empty your pockets!"

He pulled out a cell phone that was on record mode. However, it was not live streaming. It was just recording to the phone. Pretty P tapped the screen and stopped the recording. He then hit delete before slamming the phone down and breaking it.

"This piece of shit was wired for sound!" Pretty P said. "We should go ahead and put a bullet in his head."

"I'ma fucking Federal agent!" he yelled out, no longer using the fake-ass Italian accent he was portraying.

Donte fired off a thunderous round into his stomach, which knocked the wind out of him as the pain soared through his body and the burning bullet melted his flesh.

"Aggghhh! You're not going to get away with this!"

"I just did, you dumb fuck! No one was listening, and we checked the perimeter before you came. No one is waiting outside for you. You're deep undercover, and Joey either fell for your shit, or he sent you to set me up!"

Bobby V knew he could not do anything about the situation now, but he still tried to talk his way out of it.

"Donte, you can have the diamonds, just let me go! I have two kids at home waiting on me to get back."

Donte nodded his head to Road Dog, who stood up and came around the table. He tapped Skinny Pete's shoulder to release him, only to wrap his massive arms around his neck himself constricting Bobby V like a python. His legs started shaking as he struggled to be released, but to no avail. Road Dog shook Bobby V until he snapped his neck in his powerful grip, which forced the life from his flesh.

"Sal, what are you standing there for? He's dead already!" Skinny Pete said.

"I got new clothes on. What do you want me to do? I don't want his blood on this Versace shirt I just got. It cost me a lot of freaking money, you know?"

"Well you got to put in some work anyway, and we got to get rid of this prick."

"All right then, I'll take my shirt off so I don't ruin it."

They all pitched in and wrapped his body in plastic, and then duct taped the plastic to make sure the bullet wound in his stomach did not leak onto the floor.

"So what are we going to do with the body? We making him disappear or what?"

"We're going to make a statement so those miserable bastards don't try anything like this ever again. As for me, you, and Skinny Pete, we're going down to Florida to pay Joey Outlaw a visit."

CHAPTER 13

It was 3:32 p.m. in Manhattan, and Cat, Mya, and Princess were all together at the high-rise. Cat was filling them in on the juicy details of her night and morning with Don Renosa.

Princess then noticed the diamond bracelet sparkling on her wrist.

"Let me find out, ma, but are you accepting gifts for your treasure? Before you know it, you'll be down there and come back with a rock on your finger!"

"Stop playing, Princess. I like nice things just like any woman. Besides, if he put a ring on it, I'm not coming back."

"So you gonna leave us single and alone?"

Princess asked.

"You can have Jesus, and Mya can have Carlos."

"She's making plans already about how shit is going to be!" Mya began. "Jacuzzi sex got you wide open, ma. Don't be falling too fast and lose focus of what we got going on up here, especially mixing business with pleasure."

"Really, I'm not the one visually undressing Carlos, Mya. If that shit didn't happen with the AG, Carlos would still be between them legs getting you wet."

"She's got a point, Mya, because I know I would have been in every room of that mansion with Jesus's fine ass putting it down on me. But no man, on the real, is gonna come between us, Mya, and you know this. We go way back."

The ladies sat back talking, drinking, and

enjoying each other's time together now that they were on top of their game. Being in business with as much product as they were selling, they now focused on investing their cash flow into real estate, online clothing businesses, restaurants, and more to keep the money flowing far after they retired from the game.

As the ladies continued talking, the doorbell rang at the exact same time that Cat's phone went off. She picked up on the second ring and saw that it was Don Renosa calling. Princess made her way to the door and opened it, where she saw a bouquet of two dozen arranged roses. She signed for them and brought them back into the living room, where Cat lit up upon seeing them. She knew who they were from. Princess tried to grab the card to read it herself, but Cat snatched it right back from her.

"I just got the roses. Gracias, papi, for thinking of me, even with the long distance between us."

"To be honest with you and myself, Catrina, I don't allow too many people in my circle, let alone allow someone in my home as you were. However, I can trust you and welcome you into my life, and these roses are simply a gesture of me appreciating you. So I welcome you to come spend this upcoming weekend with me so we can explore my country and its beauty, and at the same time, find something in each other worth coming back to."

She started laughing and smiling hard, and her heart felt good listening to his words flow deep into her heart.

"The pleasure would be mine to see you again, papi. I'll see you this weekend, unless you can't wait, and then we'll FaceTime, and I'll try on some lingerie that you might like to see me in."

"You would make anything look good. Take care, beautiful. I'll see you then."

After the call, Cat stood up to smell the roses with a smile on her heart and face.

"Damn, ma! He got you dick-whipped. But I ain't gonna hate on you, mamacita!" Princess joked.

"He's a good person with a lot of power, and that turns me on even more. The staff provides good service, and he's giving me good sex. He looks good and has a lot of power, so what isn't there to like about this man?"

"Just be smart about it all because you my bitch. If he hurts you, I'll put him down!" Mya said.

"I got this, chica. We got this as a team. No one is going to come between us or what we have," Cat said, looking on at Mya and seeing the look in her eyes like she wanted to say more but didn't.

The world's most feared drug lord and America's most feared drug queenpin found the balance in each other, which was something no one ever expected.

CHAPTER 14

At 6:05 p.m., Joey Outlaw was at his pizzeria in Miami with his long-time goomba, Rich Scarfo, enjoying a pie and watching a newsflash about a dead FBI agent.

"This just in! FBI Agent John Smith, known in the underworld as Bobby V, has been found murdered in Manhattan. Federal authorities believe his cover was blown and may be the cause of his death that has left his wife and two children without their father. The authorities say they will not sleep until this crime is solved. I'm Ricky Wagner here at ABC News. Stay tuned for more on this study as it unfolds."

"Aye, Ricky, what do ya think about that thing

there up in the city?" Joey asked, not believing what he was seeing but knowing Donte was behind this.

Ricky Scarfo was also from the old days. He was a true gangsta and money-maker for the family. He made his bones as a teen when asked to take out a member of the Lucchese family to prove his loyalty. He stood five eight and weighed 260, a real fat pudgy guy that loved to eat. He was clean-shaven and had streaks of gray in his slicked-back black hair. He always tried to preserve his youth although he was sixty-two years old. His raspy voice was distinctive with his Italian accent.

"I tell you, Joey, from the looks of things, the kid got to him. But if he comes this way, we don't know nothing. For all we know, this guy could have gotten to us. That's what we tell 'em."

"Sounds good, but you know that kid's a loose

cannon. I may need to have a few guys come around until this thing blows over."

"Don't worry, I got the peace-maker right here. I'll deal with anybody that comes our way. Trust me! I'm not going out like that, you know?" Ricky replied as he pulled out his nickel-plated .38 snub-nose revolver.

He then displayed it before setting it back on the seat beside him for easy access.

"Maybe we should remove the kid anyway before he comes at us?"

"Well, the thing about that, Joey, is we're damned if we do and screwed if we don't, since he is one of us. We can't go around killing people without permission, because then the don will send guys our way, and that's not good either!"

"Okay, may be that wasn't too good of an idea,

but we have to come up with something here."

Joey stopped talking when he saw Skinny Pete walk through the front door with a box in his hand. Right then, Joey turned to the side door to see if Donte was coming inside, but he wasn't. Skinny Pete walked in with a smile when he noticed that Joey's sneaky rat ass was somewhat shocked by his presence. So he continued to smile to make his presence appear not as intimidating.

"Aye, paesan, look at you two getting fat down here making all of the money and getting the babes," Skinny Pete said while walking up to the table and placing a box of cannolis beside Joey Outlaw.

"So what brings you down here to Miami, Skinny Pete?" Ricky Scarfo asked.

"I was in town on business, so I figured I'd stop by and bring some of my old goombas the best cannolis in New York. Take one; it's a taste from home," he replied as he reached into the box and grabbed one for himself.

Both men looked as if they did not trust the pastries. Skinny Pete bit into his, with cream on the edges of his mouth.

"Mmmmm, this right here will take you back home, I tell ya!"

"Don't eat 'em all! You brought them for us!" Ricky joked as he reached his hand into the box and took one and chomped down on it. "These things are good, but I know you didn't go outta ya way to bring a special box of cannolis down here."

Skinny Pete put his arm around Joey Outlaw in a jovial manner and tried to break the tension that he sensed from the two scumbags.

"I miss you guys up there in the city. Anyway,

what's with this Bobby V guy? He never came by to talk to us. Is he really about his business or what?" Skinny Pete said, acting as if he knew nothing about the man that had been killed.

Joey Outlaw's heart started to beat fast when he thought he was about to get whacked just like in the old days when someone would send a friend to do the job. It would make you think all was well and then bam. Just like that, it was over! Joey was not about to let that happen to him, so he made up a quick excuse to get up.

"Geez, these friggin' pepperonis are killing my stomach. They don't agree with me like they used to. I gotta use the shitta," he said as he got up and his mind began to race as he tried to figure out his next move.

He made his way toward the bathroom. As soon

as he looked back and saw that Skinny Pete was not looking in his direction, he slid out the side door of the pizzeria and made his way over to his Lincoln Town Car. As soon as he grabbed the door, he heard Donte's voice right behind him.

"Now just where do you think you're going, fat boy? You tried to set me up, you piece of shit!"

Joey Outlaw tried to plead his way out of it as he turned around. "Donte, it's not what you think. I—!"

Donte didn't even let him try to weasel his way out of this. He pulled the trigger five times and sent multiple slugs into Joey's face and body, which spewed his brains and blood onto his pearl-white Lincoln Town Car.

Back inside the pizzeria, the gunfire alerted Ricky Scarfo, so he moved quick and grabbed his .38 snub nose beside him and fired off two rounds under the table. Skinny Pete tried to move out of the way, but still caught the slugs in his stomach. Pete didn't even have a chance to grab his gun because Ricky's fat ass was up on his feet as he made his way over to take him out. But Donte came in from behind him and fired off two thunderous rounds into the back of his head and dropped him where he stood. He then rushed over to Skinny Pete.

"Pete, you all right? We gotta get outta here!" he said as he helped him up and saw the blood on his shirt. "Not good. We gotta get you to a hospital!"

Donte helped his friend outside and into the Chevy Impala airport rental car. He mashed the gas and talked to Pete. He glanced over at him and saw that his head was leaning back against the headrest and he was clutching his stomach in pain.

"That prick got me, Donte!" Skinny Pete said.

"I got him and that rat Joey Outlaw, who tried to sneak out on ya," Donte explained as he looked over at Skinny Pete with his eyes closed and head back. "Aye, ya not gonna die on me over there, are ya?"

"I'm okay. I'll try not to die, but these bullets did a number on me!" he said, seeing and feeling the blood spewing from his stomach.

Donte drove faster toward the hospital as the cabin of the car became silent.

He mashed the gas and tried to find a hospital via his navigation system. Only a few blocks away from a hospital, Donte glanced back over at Skinny Pete and saw his head back and eyes closed, and he looked like he was peacefully sleeping. Donte slowed down before he found a place to pull over.

"Come on, Skinny Pete, you aren't supposed to die on me! We're almost at the hospital," Donte snapped.

He really respected the old-school gangsta. Pete was like a father figure to the crew, and gave them the game and wisdom they needed from the old days.

He wanted to drive back to New York with him in the car, but it was too risky, even if he wanted to look after the mobster. He did something he really did not want to do. He took his body to an alleyway and propped him up against the wall, before getting back into his car. He took a sniff of the raw cocaine powder that sent a wave of euphoric pleasure to his mind and through his body. It made him want to kill all the old guys and start a new breed of Mafia his way.

CHAPTER 15

At 8:43 the next morning, Cat was in her high-rise in Manhattan in a deep sleep on the couch across from Princess, who was asleep on the other couch. Cat's cell phone sounded off and woke her. She wiped her eyes and checked the digital clock on the wall. She also noticed that Mya was not there in the room as she scanned it, meaning she left early or after they had all fallen asleep. They stayed up watching movies the night before. She then answered the phone and heard a hyped-up Carlos.

"Good morning."

"Cat! Cat! This is Carlos, mami. They got Don Renosa. Turn on CNN News now!"

Cat's heart dropped when she heard the bad

news. She let the phone go and reached for the remote to turn on the television. The pain she felt for the man she wanted to spend her life with began to eat at her.

"Princess, wake up, mami. Look at this shit on TV!" Cat yelled as she leaned down to pick up the phone and place it on intercom. "Wait one minute, Carlos. Let me listen to what they're saying!"

As they zoomed in she saw the Colombia military and FBI escorting Don Renosa and Jesus into a jumbo jet and extraditing them to the US.

"As you can see, the notorious Don Renosa and his right-hand man, Jesus Corales, were finally in custody and being brought in on numerous counts of drug distribution. The FBI also stated that these men may be responsible for the disappearance and murder of US attorney general Geramy Lucas, an inside source says they witnessed. Don Renosa and his female companion expedited the murder," the news reporter stated, which immediately got Cat's attention, sending fear into her heart and mind that made her think about going to jail for the first time.

"Hey, Carlos, how did this happen?"

"That fucking bitch you call a friend!"

"Which friend, papi?" she asked as she looked over at Princess.

"Mya Perez! She's an undercover Federal agent! She helped bring down Don Renosa. She also told them about the AG and the tons of cocaine."

A wave of pain like knives stabbed at Cat's heart and body all at once. This was the ultimate betrayal, and it stung deep.

"That punta! No wonder she's not here. I want her dead! Oh my God! I'ma kill that bitch!" Cat snapped.

"Cat! Cat! I want you to listen to me, niña. They have Dona Renosa in a prison in San Antonio, but not for long. They'll keep moving him around, not wanting anyone to try to break him out. Anyway, go visit him and explain that you didn't know anything about this bitch because, without hesitation, he will give the order to kill her and everything she loves, including her friends. Leave New York now, and find a place where you'll be safe for a while. I'll keep in contact."

He hung up and left her to her thoughts and feelings.

"How could this bitch play us like that, ma? I'm

going to kill her for taking him away from me!"

"I'll help you take her out for this shit. She really played us, since she's known us since we was kids. She then comes back on the scene and acts like she missed us. That fucking bitch deserves all of the bullets that are coming her way!" Princess added.

It didn't take long before Cat and Princess made it to the airport and flew down to see Don Renosa. She wanted him to be free, so they could be together and in power together. Nothing else mattered.

CHAPTER 16

At 12:50 p.m., Cat and Princess made it down to the prison to see Jesus and Don Renosa. Cat was nervous and rightfully so, waiting on him to come out. She wanted him to know the truth, because Mya also had blindsided her.

The visiting area was lined with phones and thick glass that separated the visitors from the inmates.

Don Renosa walked out in an orange jump suit, a look that was far from the way she remembered him dressing. This man of power now looked helpless in her eyes behind the thick glass. She broke down in tears when she saw him. He placed his hand on the glass as he picked up the phone. He wanted to comfort her and wipe away her tears.

"Don't cry, niña, everything will be okay."

"No! No, it's not, papi! That fucking bitch betrayed my friendship and trust. She turned on you and took you away from me. I hate her for this!"

"This is my worry now. You will be okay. I promise you that we will spend the weekend together. I don't make promises or plans that I cannot keep."

Cat managed to break a smile through her pain and tears. Princess gave her a tissue to wipe her eyes.

"So what do I do until then? You know I'll come visit you wherever they send you."

He smiled thinking about her loyalty and willingness to ride for him and with him. But he did wonder if she was deceiving him, just like Mya Perez did. He sat back and smiled.

"You're beautiful even when you cry, niña! I will

miss you while I'm here. Now as far as what needs to be done, it's already in motion, so we'll be together soon."

He did not want to say too much over the phone, because he knew they recorded the visits. He placed a note up against the glass so she could read it. It was a phone number for someone named Angel de la Muerte. He was a Colombian assassin used by the cartels and some officials in high places. A second number on the paper was Don Renosa's long-time friend and real American gangsta Tom "Tommy Guns" Anderson. She memorized the names and numbers, but she needed to know what she had to do with them.

"So when they hear from me, do I tell them my story?" she asked, being slick in her wording.

"Yes, and make them aware of the cause," he

responded, referring to Mya Perez.

"I'll take care of this now, so you can come home to me. Take care, papi!"

He put his hand back on the glass and she did the same as they both looked into each other's eyes.

"I want your love in my life," she said, which brought a smile to his face.

"Real soon, niña, real soon!"

She blew him a kiss before exiting to take care of the business he had asked of her by calling the numbers of both men. She could not go back to New York, so she stopped in Harrisburg, Pennsylvania, where she got a suite at the Hilton.

Princess looked out at the night-lit skyline of the city and processed all that was going on with Mya betraying them.

"You think we good, Cat? I mean, with your boy

Don Renosa?"

"We better be. I hope he's not deceiving me with his promises. Besides, I made those calls and took care of shit for him. He knows I'm with him and not against him."

Princess walked over and hugged Cat. She felt scared for once, since she was not the boss killa that could wipe out an entire family. She had seen the power that Don Renosa possessed. It was the real deal.

"I love you, ma, and no matter what, we're gonna ride this thing all the way out!" Princess told her.

"I love you too. You know you're my number one bitch!" Cat responded, which brought laughter into the room and broke the tension they were both feeling because of all the ongoing drama.

They sat down and ordered take-out and then

watched movies until there was a knock on their hotel door.

Room service had already delivered their food, so they both looked at one another and wondered who it could be. Princess made her way over to the door and saw a Latina on the other side through the peephole.

"Hey, mami," Princess said.

"Hi, how are you? My name is Mariana Renosa."

Princess and Cat heard her say her name. At first, they thought she could be Don Renosa's ex-wife or something, until she continued to speak.

"Ricardo is my brother."

Princess opened the door, and Mariana's ride-or-die friends, Carmen and Diamond, came into view.

"Catrina, my brother thinks very highly of you, so he sent me to find you and keep you two safe."

Mariana was the exotic-looking one of the three. Her light green eyes flowed with her light Colombian skin tone. She was a distinctive beauty with long, satiny black hair that hung down the middle of her back. The mole above the center of her lips drew attention straight to her soft and plump-looking lips.

Carmen was a natural Mexican-born beauty that favored Salma Hayek. She had a curvy body and dark brown hair with golden highlights.

Diamond was a sexy chocolate girl from Miami. She could have easily been a model or video vixen, with her honey-brown eyes, heart-shaped lips to kiss, and a body of perfection and curves.

They had all met each other through the men they once loved, but who were no longer with them. Yet they still held them down even though they were dead and gone.

Mariana got straight to the point with the ladies. She told Cat and Princess that she wanted them to know that she was going to be the one that caught and killed Mya for what she had done to her brother.

"Mya, she's your friend, yes?"

"She's not my friend anymore. That bitch is a traitor!" Catrina yelled.

"Understood! This bitch must die, and I'll kill her myself," Mariana said.

"Your brother gave me info that I passed on to Tommy Guns and Angel de la Muerte."

"I do understand, but he's my brother. I feel the pain, not Tommy or Angel."

"So what is it you want from me and my girl Princess?"

"You can start by telling me where this bitch lives. If you like, you can help me and my girls torture her before we kill her."

"She was staying in Queens in an apartment, but with her being a Federal agent, that was probably her cover spot. Truth be told, it's going to be hard to get close to her now. But I'm down for tracking her," Princess explained.

"We may not get to her as we wish, but Angel de la Muerte doesn't fail! He always kills his targets!"

"In the meantime, we can try to find this bitch and put pressure on her at every angle. But right now, I'm hungry and ready to finish all of this food we ordered," Cat said.

The women ate, laughed, cried, and then got back to business before they all fell asleep thinking about getting Mya for her betrayal.

CHAPTER 17

Donte and his crew were hanging outside the deli early afternoon, minus Skinny Pete. He was now focused on taking out the old guys for trying to set him up. He knew that since Joey Outlaw had come at him, and Ricky Scarfo had backed him up, the other old guys would attempt to remove him from his position by any means as well.

"You know that thing was all over the news last night and this morning. It's a shame what happened to Skinny Pete. You know we have to figure out what we're going to do when the don comes around asking about that thing down there," Pretty P said.

"Sal, you know we can't say we know about whacking two made guys. That is an automatic death sentence. As far as I know, we saw it on the news like everyone else in America did."

"Skinny Pete, my guy, we're going to miss him around him. Too bad he had to go so soon, ya know?"

"Pretty P, hate to break it to ya, but he's not coming back. This time right now is ours to claim. We can start a new breed of Mafia with our crew and make our own rules. Besides, that stunt Jocy Outlaw pulled with that Bobby V, the don would have whacked him himself if he had found out about that," Donte informed.

"You're right, we don't need guys like that running around in this family, especially trying to gang up on us to get us out of the way," Road Dog said. "This looks like the big guy coming through," he said, when he saw the black Rolls Royce Phantom come down the street and pull up at the curb.

"Well, men, I guess we have to deal with this thing sooner rather than later," Donte said.

Pretty P whipped out his comb and ran it through his hair. He nervously watched the men in the town car step out and then walk over to the Phantom by the door.

"Donte, Don Clericuzio wants to speak with you," the Mafia goon said.

Donte got up from his chair and adjusted his clothing, and then made his way to the car. He looked on at the goons standing by. They opened the door and allowed him to get inside before shutting the door behind him. The driver stepped out but stood by for the don. He knew he wanted to have a private conversation with his grandson. Once Donte was inside the Phantom, concealed behind the dark-tinted windows and curtains, the don began to speak with a calm yet powerful tone.

"I'm going to ask you one time and one time only. What do you know about the Bobby V thing or whatever his real name was?"

Donte leaned in the corner of the back seat and then looked back at the don. He was not expecting that question.

"I know what's been on the news about this guy being a Federal agent or something like that, and he was found dead."

Don Clericuzio did not even look at Donte. Instead, he was watching the news on the television in the headrest with the volume down.

"So nothing on that thing, huh? What about Joey

Outlaw and Ricky Scarfo?"

"I heard somebody got to them, and it didn't end so good."

The don now turned his head and looked into Donte's face and eyes. He began to speak, since he was upset about the events that had taken place, especially since two of his cops and a lieutenant had been murdered.

"See, it's kind of hard for me to believe that you don't know anything about this considering that Skinny Pete, one of your guys, was also found dead down there. I bet when the forensics details come back, the bullets from Ricky's gun were the ones fired into Skinny Pete. Now if I'm wrong about what I'm suspecting, this means this family is about to go to war because two of my capos are dead."

"I tell ya, it's a shame what happened to Skinny Pete. He was the wisdom and balance to my crew. I will have my guys look into this thing because war takes away from money being made, you know, and that's not good for no one involved."

As the don sat and listened to his grandson, he felt that Donte was going to become a problem that could hurt the family, just like John Gotti became to the Gambino family and name. He also caught wind of Donte's side drug dealings, which was another Mafia no-no. He did not bother to question him about it, because he knew he would deny it.

"You can excuse yourself now," the don said, without even looking at him.

Donte wanted to strangle the old man right then and there, especially knowing he would come for him or he might try to have one of his goons standing outside of the car try something. He was ready either way.

Donte stepped out of the car and turned around to see his grand-pop still looking at the screen. He was noticeably pissed. Right then he knew that his time was coming to an end, along with his crew's.

The don and his men pulled off and left Donte to vent to his crew about what had just taken place inside the car.

"Aye, we all have to be on the lookout. This old piece of shit may be gunning for us. He asked me about the Bobby V thing and then about the situation down in Miami. I told him I didn't know a thing other than what I had heard on the news. Forget about it! He thinks I'm going to let him come at me. We can take out his old ass and run this family."

"Donte, I'll have my guys from Brooklyn come over this way. They love putting in work," Road Dog said.

"We can handle that later, because I do want to teach this old prick a lesson. Sal, you can help with this thing, too. Road Dog, put your guys on standby," Donte vented as his mind started putting all of the pieces together for the takeover of the family.

CHAPTER 18

Around 3:15 p.m. in Woodlawn, Maryland, Janice Perez, a forty-nine-year-old grandmother and mother of Mya Perez, was walking with her grandson, who loved the oversized lollipop she had just bought him at the candy store. He did not have a care in the world while he enjoyed the sweet pleasure. As they got closer to her house, Janice noticed two Federal agents sitting in a car out in front on the cul de sac. She immediately started to think that something was wrong with her daughter, Mya, so she ran up to the car and wanted to know what was going on.

"Agents Davis and Hernandez, is everything okay with my daughter?"

"Yes, ma'am, we've just been assigned here until this major case she's involved in blows over."

"Okay, I guess I'll be feeding you guys since you'll be away from your families. I'll be back out within an hour to bring you some home-cooked love," she said, making her way back to the house.

About twenty minutes later, Mya pulled up in her personal vehicle, a Honda Accord. She, too, noticed the agents' presence.

"Hey, guys, thank you for being here. It'll make it a lot easier for me to sleep knowing you two are on the job," she said with a smile.

"Seeing your sexy self makes our job a lot easier," Agent Davis joked and flirted.

She made her way into the house. Upon entry, she noticed a boyish-looking man squatting down and playing with her son. He made him laugh. However, he was someone Mya had never seen before.

"Excuse me, papi. I'm Mya, are you here with my mom?"

Miguel Sanchez was also known in the underworld as Angel de la Muerte, and it was he who was playing with her son in her mother's living room. Little did she know that her end was very near. No one ever expects to meet death when he's around, until it's too late.

"Yes, mami. I'm your mother's friend."

"Where is my mother?"

"In the kitchen preparing food for the men outside," he said as he picked up Mya's son and walked over toward the kitchen behind her.

COST OF BETRAYAL 2

As soon as she entered the kitchen, she was greeted with the sight of her mother's body slumped over the kitchen table with her brains blown out. Blood had mixed in with the food she was preparing on the table. In the split seconds it took for her to process it all, Miguel already had a gun drawn on her and placed his silenced 9 mm up against her head.

"Don't be stupid, niña, because I will blow your son's head off. Now, get on your knees and put your hands behind your head," he ordered calmly yet with control.

Miguel stood five eleven, weighed 170 pounds, and had black hair with blonde highlights. He was casually dressed in the latest name-brand fashions with a feminine touch. Although he was an outspoken gay man, he was also a stone-cold killer that never hesitated to complete the job given to him.

"You know why I'm here. You crossed the wrong person, Don Renosa, which cost your mother her life. I wanted you to know this before I take yours. It's a shame because you are beautiful but deadly in so many ways," he said as he let her son run to her.

She embraced him with a hug full of love, and then she closed her eyes to embrace what was to come next.

Miguel pointed his weapon at her with her eyes closed as if to embrace the pain of hugging her son with love one last time. Then it happened. He squeezed off a round into her son's head, killing him instantly. At the same time, she felt the bullet that just had hit him, because it passed through him and went into her flesh. Her eyes opened in disbelief just as her mouth was ready to scream out, until he fired off two more silenced rounds. One flew into her open mouth and the other into the center of her head, ejecting chunks of brain out the other side. He turned around and tucked his weapon against the small of his back under his silk, baby-blue Prada shirt before he made his way out of the house as if nothing had happened.

As soon as he stepped out of the house, the Federal agents both spotted him. Agent Davis tapped his partner on the shoulder.

"Look at this guy coming from inside. How did he get in there without us seeing him go in?" Davis said, feeling as if he and his partner missed out on his entrance because they were in deep conversation about the case.

Each agent jumped out of the car and wanted to approach the boyish-looking man to find out who he was and how and when he entered the home.

Miguel saw them approaching fast, so he went into diva mode.

"What are you doing coming from inside that house? We didn't see you go in."

"Maybe because you weren't looking at me, big man. How could you miss all of this?" Miguel said, turning his homo all the way up.

"What! What's your name and relation to Mya? I don't know you and have never seen you before," Agent Davis questioned.

"Mmmmm, you just calm down, big man with them big ol' arms all over the place. She's my people."

Agent Davis's face turned up at the homo's attempt to be freaky with him. At the same time, he did not believe a word he was saying about this relationship with Mya, so he started to run toward the house and call out for her.

Agent Hernandez also did not like Miguel's roaming eyes, which made him feel very uncomfortable. However, it was a distraction. Even as Agent Davis took off running and yelling, his partner briefly shifted this head and looked his way, only to give Miguel enough time to remove his silenced 9 mm pistol. He shot Agent Hernandez in the face, which snapped his neck back as the force of the slug twisted his body around and killed him where he stood as he fell to the ground.

In the same swift motion, he fired multiple

rounds through the air toward Agent Davis, which tracked him down and crashed into his legs, arm, and vest. The force of the slugs dropped the large agent, yet his fear of being killed and the flow of adrenaline rushing through his body gave him the strength to bounce back to his feet. He immediately reached for his sidearm, but he was not fast enough.

"No, no, no, big man! I can't let you do that!" Miguel said as he fired off two more shots into the agent's face, which killed him instantly.

Miguel turned and saw the curtain move on the house across the street. But he did not bother tending to the nosey neighbors. Instead, he calmly walked away as if nothing was wrong with what he had just done. This Colombian assassin was true to his word: Never leave a job unfinished.

CHAPTER 19

At 5:20 p.m., Don Clericuzio and the heads of the four other families were at Pauly Fingers's old restaurant in the Bronx to discuss the matters of the death of his men: Skinny Pete, Ricky Scarfo, and Joey Outlaw.

Fat Tommy "Thumbs" Gambino, of the Gambino family; Tony "G" Giancana, of the Lucchese family; Michael "The Black Hand" Merlino; and Vinnie "the Chin" Genovese had all joined Don Clericuzio to enjoy the five-star Italian cuisine, along with fresh garlic bread dipped in virgin olive oil and fine red wine from the old country.

"Gentlemen, gentlemen!" Don Clericuzio said, getting everyone's attention as he sipped his red wine to clear the food in his mouth before addressing the commission.

All the other bosses looked on to see what the capo dei capi had to say.

"I hope you're all enjoying this fine food. But as you know, this gathering is more than good food and conversation. I brought you all here to address the situation down in Miami. No names needed, but I'm quite sure all of us here watch the news and have our ears to the streets. I just want to make sure that none of your guys had a hand in this!"

As the don spoke, he scanned the room and looked at each of the faces and their demeanor, but saw nothing that would tell him they knew anything.

"I take it that nobody here knows anything?"

They all shook their heads no. Then Fat Tommy

"Thumbs" began to speak. "Don Clericuzio, you might have to look within your own family, because none of us here want problems like that. It's not good for growth or business. The word on the streets is that your grandson, Donte, is a loose cannon, so maybe check with him. No disrespect, but it's what's out there on the streets."

The other bosses continued to eat as Don Clericuzio grabbed his glass of wine before responding to Fat Tommy "Thumbs."

"So you think it's inside of my family, huh?"

Tommy "Thumbs" got his nickname by how he interlocked his fingers and twirled his thumbs when he was thinking or was nervous, and it became a habit.

"It's what the word on the streets is right now.

Like I said, I mean no disrespect."

But Don Clericuzio knew he had a problem with Donte. He just wanted to make sure it was not an outside source that took out his men. Being in this situation was embarrassing to go through as a don, which meant his grandson had to go.

As he started to speak, the front door swung open and in walked Donte, Road Dog, Pretty P, and twenty of Road Dog's Brooklyn goons strapped with AR-15s, 9 mm Uzis, TEC-9s, and hand guns ready for whatever. The Mafia bosses and their security teams were all caught off guard, especially Donte Clericuzio, when he saw his grandson leading the way. When the don saw this, he realized it was going to turn bad fast, and perhaps even worse than what had happened to Paul Castellano when John Gotti wanted to take over the family.

Donte gripped his twin 10 mm Colts with black pearl handles.

"Don Clericuzio, I'm taking over this family now! I'm going to run it with a new direction. Like you said to me months ago, I am the future of this family!"

"So, what are ya gonna do, start a friggin' family with a bunch of mulis?" Vinnie "the Chin" asked sarcastically, which offended Donte and his men.

However, Road Dog also took offense, so he took his .45 automatic and pumped two rounds into the back of Vinnie's head, instantly slumping him as his brains and warm blood sprayed across the table, as his face fell into the plate of spaghetti he was eating. The sudden gunfire startled the other bosses, yet it did get their attention.

Michael "the Black Hand" Merlino made it clear to Donte and his crew that he did not want war or any problems with them.

"Donte, your problems don't affect me or my family; and no disrespect to you, Don Clericuzio, but this war is your problem!"

"You're right, Don Merlino. Do you agree, Don Gambino and Don Giancana?"

"Yeah, Donte, like I said, this is his problem. Donte is more of a force to be reckoned with. So my problem isn't with you, Donte, so I'm outta this thing here."

Donte then shifted both guns into his grandfather's face. "I am the future, so your reign ends here and now. Say hello to Uncle Pauly for me," he said as he fired off multiple slugs into the old man's face and body, not only to kill him but also to make a statement to the other dons sitting around the table. This power move he just did made him the capo dei capi—the boss of all bosses. "I'm in charge of this thing of ours now. The boss of all bosses! You all can side with me or die right now! I'm running everything with new order, so you either like it or not!"

As those words flowed from Donte's mouth, Pretty P came up behind the other dons and put a bullet in the back of each of their heads, one by one. None of them ever saw how quickly he moved.

"We got to start fresh. We can't trust these old guys. They smile in your face and then, bam, they whack ya just like that. So, we beat 'em to it!" Pretty

P said.

Donte smirked, appreciating the move his long-time friend had just made. He already knew he would make his friend the underboss.

"Road Dog, have your team take care of the rest of these guys," Donte ordered, referring to the security.

They were all in shock and knew that any attempt to reach for their guns would only expedite their deaths.

Donte, Pretty P, and Road Dog all exited the restaurant, leaving behind the gang-land-style massacre and feeling the power shift. Al Capone himself would have been impressed with how this all played out.

The FBI sat in their car down the street from the

restaurant. They knew the five heads were meeting there today. They had them under surveillance, especially when they were all together. However, when the gunfire erupted, they wanted to move in, knowing who they had seen walk inside, but they were outnumbered. Also, the city police would have run into a trap with these young goons not valuing life—even their own. The Feds did not see this coming, yet ridding themselves of these bosses would put an end to the cases they were building against them.

CHAPTER 20

The picturesque sun was setting at 7:45, and assisted the powder blue that was fading into the Miami nightlife.

Carlos Rodriguez was leaving the police station after a long day of being interrogated by Internal Affairs about his association with Don Renosa and Jesus Corales. He denied any relations with them at all. He even denied knowing them other than what he had seen and heard on television.

He came out of the station, hopped into his Ferrari, and headed back to his place to get rested for the day ahead. He was working an undercover case with some Jamaicans that wanted to exchange kilos of cocaine for hundreds of pounds of marijuana.

As Rodriguez drove back to his place, he thought about Don Renosa. He knew that if the don ever found out about him speaking with Internal Affairs, he would be paranoid and have someone take him out just because, especially after he had been arrested.

Carlos came to a red light and was still in thought when his cell phone sounded off and got his attention. As it was ringing, a CL65 Mercedes Benz pulled up alongside him as he answered his phone. The light turned green, but he did not pull off at that very moment. He looked to his left as he spoke into the phone. "What's up? Who is this?"

The person on the phone was in the Mercedes right beside him, but he did not know who it was.

"Carlos, papi, looks like you had a long day. I think you need some rest, for good."

"Who the fuck are you, and how did you get my number, crazy ass?"

"Angel de la Muerte. Rest in peace!"

As those words came out of Miguel's mouth, he floored the pedal of the CL65 Benz and forced the V12 engine to thrust him away fast and far enough so he could detonate the mounted C-4 explosives beneath the driver's side of Carlos's car. It erupted with a flash of fire and ground-shaking force that roared loud through the city streets and shattered windows from the blast, yet engulfed Carlos in flames that burned him to a crisp.

Miguel smiled as he continued to drive off. He then weaved in and out of traffic as he headed to his next assignment.

Don Renosa made sure he covered all of his

tracks, leaving no association with Mya to survive, even his associates, except for Jesus, his right-hand man and trusted goon.

Don Renosa was a man of strategic intelligence and never placed all his eggs in one basket, which is why he sent another message to Miguel through his sister, Mariana. She, too, wanted to see her big brother freed by any means that fell within the code of this business.

CHAPTER 21

Two days later, Donte and his crew all sat outside the deli reflecting back to the dons' faces when they came through the door and how it all had gone down. Road Dog was also present with over twenty of his young thugs from Brooklyn, since everyone was on high alert because they had killed the dons. The underbosses of those families might try to make a move if they found out who was responsible. Donte and his team were ready either way.

Little did Donte know that the FBI was watching him and his crew from both afar and up close. Some of the customers inside and outside the deli were awaiting their cue to move in and take them all down.

Donte was high on the raw cocaine he had

snorted every few minutes, which made him paranoid, especially with all that had been going on. He snorted the cocaine discreetly from the valve that he was clenching in his fist. It only made him look around and check everyone out, thinking something was going on.

"Aye, Sal. What's up with that van down there? I never seen it before."

"What van you ya talking about, Donte?" Sal asked.

"That blue custom van. If it was a snake, it would have bitten ya already. Jesus Christ!"

"I don't know what you want me to do. Should I send one of the Brooklyn guys down there to check it out?"

"No, I want you to friggin' pose or wait until we all get whacked! Of course I want you to send someone down there. It'll make me feel better!"

"All right already, I'm on it. Hey, young buck, go check on that van down there and see what the story is with it."

The Brooklyn kid took a walk down the street and kept his gun in his waistline ready to rock out.

Donte looked to the sky and saw a helicopter flying overhead before taking off, which made him even more paranoid.

"I was about to unload on that chopper! I swear if it would have stayed a second longer, a full clip would have taken that thing right down!"

The Brooklyn thug came up on the van and saw movement inside through the front window. His senses heightened and made him pull out his Glock 9 mm. He walked to the side of the van to get a better view. Right then the side door slid open and exposed

Federal agents with their guns pointed at him. The thug was not about to let the Feds get the drop on Donte or Road Dog, so he started firing off slugs into one of the agent's chest. However, the other agents returned fire that slammed into the thug's body and instantly sucked the life out of him.

Donte jumped up quickly and reached for his gun.

"I knew that fucking van wasn't right! They want war, let's give it to them!"

The Federal agents inside and out were alerted to what was going on, so they all started identifying themselves with hopes of taking these thugs down, to no avail. This was going to be a shootout.

"Fuck all of you pigs!" Donte yelled out as he squeezed the trigger and fired on the agents who made themselves known.

Slugs returned and slammed into Donte, dropping him, but it did not stop his trigger finger from firing rounds from his downed position.

Pretty P got gunned down while he was concerned how he looked, while bullets were flying everywhere. Slugs crashed into his frame and sucked the life out of him.

Road Dog killed a few agents before he was caught in the mouth with slugs as he was yelling while firing his weapon. The young Brooklyn thugs saw their boss go down, so they shifted their weapons onto the agents that had fired on Road Dog and killed them both dead.

A slew of agents arrived in their cars and jumped out to join the gun battle. They were able to take down the Brooklyn goons using their trained skills.

Donte was so coked up that he thought he was

invincible, and he jumped up to his feet and fired off multiple shots that hit agents off guard. Suddenly, a barrage of bullets from Federal agents slammed into Donte's stomach and dropped him, after puncturing his lungs and breaching his stomach.

"Fuck! Fuck all of you! I run this shit!" he screamed out as the life escaped this real American gangster, the capo dei capi.

This crime scene looked like something from a movie set; however, those dead would not be getting a second chance to act out their violent rage. Donte and his crew lived as gangsters all the way until the end. Being in a jail cell for the rest of their lives was not in the cards for them.

It did not take long before news reporters and social media blogs reported what they had seen and heard about this gang-land-style shootout.

"This is Paul Kalune with FOX News. I'm told Donte Clericuzio, the new boss of bosses, was the man responsible for this gang-land-style massacre of Federal agents that led to his death as well. The FBI says he was far more notorious a gangster than Al Capone and John Gotti Sr. put together. Over thirty bodies lay dead here in one of the largest shootouts in New York history involving Federal agents and the Mafia. This crime scene will be talked about for years to come. More details and names of the others at eleven!"

The reporter and remaining FBI agents took in this tableau sight, having never seen anything like it in their lives. Donte Clericuzio was the last official don of what Mafia remained in this country. He would be remembered just as the gangsters in this business before him.

CHAPTER 22

Princess was in the hotel suite in Harrisburg watching the news unfold about Donte and his team. Cat was out picking up subs from the Sandwich Man down the street.

Princess was tripping off of how Donte and his crew went out gangster style by shooting it out with the Feds.

"Them dumbasses are crazy on some boss Mafia shit!" she laughed while watching the television.

Her moment was interrupted when a knock came across the door of the suite.

"Bitch, use your key card!" Princess shouted, since she was glued to the news.

She thought it was Cat at the door until another

knock came across. She put her guns into her waistline and walked to the door. Once she was at the door, she looked through the peephole and saw a guy with black hair and blonde highlights. He was wearing a pink silk shirt and white linen pants.

"Who is it?"

"Miguel, mamacita, open the door, diva. I'm here to see Catrina."

Princess started laughing at his flare. She was entertained by his full-fledged personality, so she opened the door. He walked right past her and strutted like a diva as if he was on a runway.

"Okay, mamacita, do your thing," Princess said encouragingly.

Miguel took a few more steps before he turned around and revealed his twin silencer 9 mms. Right then the smile dissipated fast from Princess's face as she reacted and reached for her .380s. But Miguel got off two shots that hit her in the arm and shoulder. She stumbled back from being hit by the slugs, feeling the brute force and pain.

"Hey, dumbass. What the fuck is this about?"

"It's a shame, mami, all of your beauty is going to waste."

Miguel came at her with a diabolical smirk on his face with his guns still aimed directly at her.

"Get down on your knees and don't be stupid!" he ordered her, but with a face more serious than the one he gave her to get into the room. His feminine tone even changed slightly to a masculine one.

Princess felt the pain emotionally and physically, since she knew her end was near.

"My name is Angel de la Muerte. I come here on behalf of Don Renosa. He wants everything cleaned up. You and anyone associated with Mya. I killed her son, her mother, and then her. You should have seen the look on her face!"

A tear slid down Princess's face as she closed her eyes. She also tensed up as if to brace herself for the end.

"If you kill her, I'll murder you a thousand times over!" Cat threatened as she came into the room.

She was alert when she saw that the door was still propped open, which made her pull out her nickel-plated 9 mm with the safety off and ready to kill.

Angel then shifted his attention to Cat when he saw that she had dropped in on him.

"Mmmm, you are without a doubt as beautiful as

I expected, but if you don't drop your gun, this pretty girl right here is dead. I'm here to do a job. I never fail."

"There's a first time for everything!"

"Is there, niña?"

He did not give her a chance to respond. He just fired the round into the center of Princess's head, which abruptly snapped her head back as the force of the slug pushed its way out the other side of her body as her life escaped her.

Cat reacted just as fast. She squeezed off multiple slugs that chased him down as he ran and dove onto the other side of the bed, where her bullets found him and crashed into his stomach and groin area.

"Aghhhh, bitch! You got me in the webels, punta!"

"I'm going to make you pay for what you did to my girl. We didn't have anything to do with what Mya did. I would have killed her myself if I had known what she was into."

Miguel lay in between the beds clenching his gun. He knew he needed to get out of there because this was not going to go well. He raised his gun and fired off blind rounds that missed Cat. She moved quickly and positioned herself to get a better aim at him. She ran and jumped up onto the bed, standing over him and catching him off guard.

"I told you, fag! This is for my girl!" she yelled, dumping the entire clip into his face and body and making him flop on the floor from the pounding of the bullets tearing through his flesh.

Cat jumped down off the bed and knew she could

not stay long. She made her way over to Princess and got down on her knees and cried over her lifeless body. She then kissed her lips.

"I love you, mami! I'm going to make them all pay for this!" Cat warned, kissing her one more time before making her escape and leaving the city in search of Don Renosa for his betrayal and turning his back on her heart as well as her loyalty toward him in business.

Don Renosa knew how vicious Cat was; however, he did not expect for this scenario to fail as it did. Like Cat said, there's a first time for everything!

CHAPTER 23

At 10:36 a.m., news reporters were all outside the San Antonio County Jail awaiting the release of Don Renosa and his associate, Jesus Corales. Their release came unexpectedly, and word spread fast that the US government was letting them go and transporting them back to Colombia for their government to deal with them. Most people knew they would eventually be released because of who they were and what they meant to their country.

They came out handcuffed and escorted by FBI agents. The new crews hounded and shoved each other while trying to get the best positions for their cameras and microphones.

"Don Renosa, did you pay your way out of this

situation?"

"Is your government going to release you once you're home?"

"Are you going to distribute cocaine to this country after this?"

"Don Renosa! Don Renosa! Did you ever have anyone killed in connection with this case?"

A smirk appeared across Don Renosa's face as the media tossed questions his way that he ignored. Tommy Guns had taken care of things for him and talked to some powerful people, including giving the president $25 million to make this all go away. He also promised the president and his associates a reasonable percentage of his cocaine distribution to this country.

As Don Renosa and Jesus continued to walk

toward the tinted Yukon Denalis that waited to take them to the airport, another question came through the air which got the don's attention.

"Hey, Ricardo! Did you really think Angel de la Muerte would kill all of us?"

Hearing Miguel's name called out in public from a familiar voice sent a wave of fear through this tough man, as he turned toward the woman asking the question. Right then he locked eyes with Catrina "Kitty Cat" Alverez. His mouth was open in disbelief. He knew that he had fucked up by betraying her. In that split second of seeing her and trying to process what to say or do, she raised the 9 mm automatic with speed and fired off slugs into his face, before shifting and firing off rounds onto Jesus. Each man was dead before their bodies hit the ground or any of the agents had time to process what had just taken place. Then, as if time had sped up seconds later, all the FBI agents swarmed Catrina and took her down and quickly disarmed her.

The cameras were still rolling as the reporters were all telling their version of what had just taken place. They were also trying to figure out who the shooter was. Millions were tuned in live watching this all unfold. Cat was now on the ground crying from the emotions she was feeling from the loss of her brother, Princess, and even the man she loved, who she had just killed, after he did not trust her enough to let her live. It was the ultimate betrayal on his behalf, so she had to make him pay.

In her eyes, the way she had seen the two of them together, they would have taken the drug world by storm. Even a bigger deal to her was that they could have been a power couple. Now she had to live with the decision she had made as well as the decision that Flaco had made that set this entire chain of events into motion.

Tommy Guns was in his mansion off the coast of Mexico watching all of this unfold on the news. He could not believe that his good associate was killed on live TV. He thought of going after her or sending word to have her dealt with, but he did not want to risk coming back to America.

Mariana took it hard when she saw her brother killed on television, as she sat thinking that he was coming home and then this happened. The staff at the compound was trying to calm her down, but she wanted blood. She wanted to see Catrina dead for this.

The agents held Cat down on the ground and whispered into her ear.

"You just did the world and most of America a favor. I can pull some strings to get you less time."

Cat did not care about less or more time. Everything that meant anything to her was now dead. She was numb from all the pain she felt and the thoughts she had. He had deceived her with a smile, which made it hurt the most when she came face-to-face with Miguel, the same person she had called for Don Renosa. Cat would never be free from the pain she felt and endured over the last year. Besides, she did not have anyone with whom to enjoy her freedom.

CHAPTER 24

Almost thirteen months later, Catrina was prepared to go to trial. Not that she wanted to; she would have rather pled out and gotten it over with. But the trial was really for the media and public.

While she spent time in prison over the last year, all the women looked up to her as the queenpin after everything they had heard about her. The media outlets, publishing companies, and movie studies all wanted to take the story of her life and tell it their way with her permission. They wanted to know how her life was with Don Renosa and more. However, she declined all the offers, because she did not want to glorify the life she lived and the one she now hated, because of the way it had turned out. Besides, she did not want a bunch of actors portraying her or her brother. It would have reminded her of the great pain she had gone through.

The entertainment producers were not the only ones that reached out to her. She also received mail with threats on her life. She disregarded these letters, but she knew she was good in jail and respected by all those around her.

However, she did have strong feeling from the sender of the letters. Mariana, Don Renosa's sister, or someone on her team, had every right to be mad, just as Cat had every right to do what she did by taking him out. Because if he found out that Miguel was killed, he would have hired another assassin to finish the job.

Cat was escorted to the courthouse with three

sheriff cars in transit. She was in the middle car looking on at the city of San Antonio as they passed through the crowds to make their way downtown.

When they arrived at the courthouse, news crews, cameras, and reporters from all over were waiting to catch a glimpse of Catrina, since it had been some time since they had seen her.

The cars all slowed down so they would not run over anyone running around in the streets. The other sheriffs at the courthouse came out from the entrance over to the cars. As soon as they opened the door and Catrina stepped out, the reporters all started yelling out.

"Catrina. Ms. Alverez. Do you think they'll be easy on you?"

"Ms. Alverez! Ms. Alverez! How true is it that

you were offered millions of dollars for your story?"

"Catrina! Do you fear for your life since Mariana Renosa is now running the Colombian cartel?"

She ignored all of the questions up until that point because her instincts gave her a bad vibe that something was wrong. So she scanned the people and surroundings around her as she entered the courthouse.

Once in the holding cell, she processed her thoughts on all that was going on around her. The trial itself was emotionally and mentally draining, especially having to relive the events all over again.

"Ms. Alverez, it's time," the sheriff said as he fondled the handcuffs and made them click over and over.

She walked up to the gate and allowed herself to

be cuffed, before they took her up to the courtroom. As she entered the courtroom, she scanned all of the faces inside to make sure that there was no one there who would give her a hard time.

"All rise for the Honorable Judge Todd J. Hoover."

Those in the courtroom stood before the judge seated everyone.

"Are all parties present here today to proceed?" the judge questioned.

"Yes, Your Honor," the defense said.

"Yes, Your Honor," the prosecution replied.

Both sides acknowledged the judge and showed that they were prepared for the largest trial in years.

As the district attorney opened with his arguments, Cat sat back but still had a feeling that something was not right, especially when she glanced up at the sheriff and saw him looking over at something or someone. So her eyes followed his, only to see what he was staring at. Mariana, Diamond, Carmen, and another female were all wearing black, even black lipstick and black eyeliner, to symbolize death.

Catrina could not take her eyes off of them, especially when she saw them quickly approach in her direction. For a few seconds, she was frozen in the moment that this could not be happening to her, until Mariana reached under her dress and pulled out a 9 mm short-stock Uzi. Right then, Cat turned to the crooked sheriff coming toward her. She jumped up and kicked him in his nuts as hard as she could, which forced him to bend over in pain. This gave her just enough time to take his sidearm. The sudden movement also caught Mariana off guard. Even their presence shocked the reporters and courtroom staff. The sheriffs that were not paid off by Mariana tried to take her out, until she and her girls gunned them all down with fully automatic weapons. Cat fired off three rounds, the first one which grazed Diamond in the shoulder. The other two hissed past Mariana's head, which enraged her even more.

Cat ran toward the door that she had entered the room through, but one of the crooked sheriffs jumped in front of her, only to be greeted with a slug to the face that dropped him. Now his body was in the way of the exit, so she dropped down to the floor out of the line of fire and pulled his body away. Most of the people inside the courtroom that were not with

Mariana were screaming, but some also were filming with their cell phones. Others just tried to stay down and not get killed.

Mariana was still coming with her team and shooting out with the other sheriffs that were now rushing into the courtroom to assist the others.

"Catrina, I'm going to kill you for what you did to my brother!" Mariana yelled out as she ran toward Cat.

But Cat jumped up and fired off rounds that slammed into Mariana's body, which thrust her back onto the defense table wounded and in pain.

Diamond, Carmen, and Jesus's sister saw this, so they focused on the sheriffs coming through the door, so they could get to Cat.

"Diamond, go after that bitch. We'll take care of

the cops!" Carmen ordered.

Diamond quickly closed in on Cat as she squeezed off her twin black steel 9 mm with extended clips.

Cat's heart raced even faster when she saw Diamond come her way, so she reached up for the handle of the door and at the same time squeezed off another burst of rounds to slow down Diamond. She then slipped into the stairwell.

Diamond dove behind the seat in the courtroom and evaded Cat's gunfire.

"Carmen! She went through that door!"

Diamond got back up and fired on the sheriffs as they all backed up and made their way into the door that Cat had gone through. The sheriffs were not so quick running behind her as they entered the stairwell, because they did not want to be ambushed. Instead, they radioed more sheriffs into the building.

"That bitch killed Mariana!" Mariana's sister, Amina, shouted.

"We can't leave her behind like that!" Diamond said.

"We can't get caught either. We came to get Catrina. If we don't get her, then we failed Mariana anyway!" Carmen said, taking control of the situation.

As those words flowed from her mouth, they heard Mariana scream out.

"She's not dead!" Diamond said, upon hearing her friend's scream followed by a barrage of gunfire that killed as many sheriffs as she could before they gunned her down.

When they got to the top of the steps, they could hear multiple sets of feet rumbling across the floor. They moved quickly through the halls, until Cat popped out of the jury holding room with her gun aimed. She had the drop on them.

"You tried to kill the wrong bitch!" Cat voiced, which got their attention.

They all turned around but not fast enough. Cat squeezed off rounds that pounded slugs into Amina and Diamond, which gave Carmen enough time to react and return fire, forcing Cat back into the room. Cat popped out the clip and saw how many rounds she had left. One round remained, which gave her one shot to end it all.

"You got my girls, but you missed me, punta!" Carmen yelled out.

Diamond and Amina were wounded badly and held their hands over their wounds.

Cat popped back into the hallway and fired off her last round, but she missed Carmen. At the same time, Carmen squeezed the trigger on her gun, only to hear a clicking sound that it was empty. Right then, Carmen's instincts told her to grab one of her girl's guns; however, just as those thoughts entered her mind, loud voices of approaching sheriffs and police officers could be heard. Both women looked at each other with murderous eyes, yet silently they came to a momentary truce to escape the courthouse. Carmen ran off, dipped into another stairwell, and took off all the black clothing she had on. She striped down to just a white T-shirt and blue jeans and let her hair down. Diamond and Amina took their guns and fired off at the approaching sheriffs. They were going to go out ride or die.

Cat slipped into the bathroom, only to walk in on a janitor. She then quickly improvised a plan.

"I don't want to shoot you, but I will. Take off all of your clothing."

The janitor did just as she had ordered. She knew who she was from watching all of the media coverage. Cat got dressed in the janitor's uniform and also took her hat and tucked her hair beneath it. She then took the cleaning cart and pushed it through the halls. She made it to the elevator and saw a sheriff step off.

"Hurry up and get out of here. Shots are being fired!" he yelled at Cat, thinking she was a janitor.

Cat made her way down the stairs and then out of

the courthouse. At the same time she spotted Carmen, who saw her as well. They both turned and blended in with the streets of San Antonio and never looked back.

Chaos filled the courthouse, as even a SWAT team arrived to contain what was left of the crime scene.

The camera crews caught as much as they could in between ducking down and taking cover. No cameras caught Cat slipping out of the courthouse. This enraged the sheriffs. She was now going to be America's most wanted notorious queenpin and murderer. She would never look back. She would have to change her identity, face, and hair and blend in and stay low somewhere. Money would not be an issue now, because she had plenty of it stashed in many places throughout New York City. She also had family and friends who no one would expect to hold her down. No matter what hood she landed in, they would all respect her gangster. To the eyes of those looking on and chasing behind her—the local, state, and Federal authorities—Catrina "Kitty Cat" Alverez had disappeared. Poof! Just like that, the queen bitch was gone!

order books, please fill out the order form below:
order films please go to www.good2gofilms.com

ame: _____

ddress:_____

ty: _____ State: _____ Zip Code: _____

one:_____

nail:_____

ethod of Payment: Check   VISA   MASTERCARD

edit Card#:_ _____

ame as it appears on card: _____

gnature: _____

tem Name	Price	Qty	Amount
8 Hours to Die – Silk White	$14.99		
Hustler's Dream - Ernest Morris	$14.99		
Hustler's Dream 2 - Ernest Morris	$14.99		
Thug's Devotion – J. L. Rose and J. M. McMillon	$14.99		
ll Eyes on Tommy Gunz – Warren Holloway	$14.99		
lack Reign – Ernest Morris	$14.99		
loody Mayhem Down South – Trayvon Jackson	$14.99		
loody Mayhem Down South 2 – Trayvon Jackson	$14.99		
usiness Is Business – Silk White	$14.99		
usiness Is Business 2 – Silk White	$14.99		
usiness Is Business 3 – Silk White	$14.99		
ash In Cash Out – Assa Raymond Baker	$14.99		
ash In Cash Out 2 - Assa Raymond Baker	$14.99		
hildhood Sweethearts – Jacob Spears	$14.99		
hildhood Sweethearts 2 – Jacob Spears	$14.99		
hildhood Sweethearts 3 - Jacob Spears	$14.99		
hildhood Sweethearts 4 - Jacob Spears	$14.99		
onnected To The Plug – Dwan Marquis Williams	$14.99		
onnected To The Plug 2 – Dwan Marquis Williams	$14.99		
onnected To The Plug 3 – Dwan Williams	$14.99		
ost of Betrayal – W.C. Holloway	$14.99		
ost of Betrayal 2 – W.C. Holloway	$14.99		
eadly Reunion – Ernest Morris	$14.99		
ream's Life – Assa Raymond Baker	$14.99		
lipping Numbers – Ernest Morris	$14.99		

Flipping Numbers 2 – Ernest Morris	$14.99		
He Loves Me, He Loves You Not - Mychea	$14.99		
He Loves Me, He Loves You Not 2 - Mychea	$14.99		
He Loves Me, He Loves You Not 3 - Mychea	$14.99		
He Loves Me, He Loves You Not 4 – Mychea	$14.99		
He Loves Me, He Loves You Not 5 – Mychea	$14.99		
Killing Signs – Ernest Morris	$14.99		
Kings of the Block – Dwan Willams	$14.99		
Kings of the Block 2 – Dwan Willams	$14.99		
Lord of My Land – Jay Morrison	$14.99		
Lost and Turned Out – Ernest Morris	$14.99		
Love & Dedication – W.C. Holloway	$14.99		
Love Hates Violence – De'Wayne Maris	$14.99		
Love Hates Violence 2 – De'Wayne Maris	$14.99		
Love Hates Violence 3 – De'Wayne Maris	$14.99		
Love Hates Violence 4 – De'Wayne Maris	$14.99		
Married To Da Streets – Silk White	$14.99		
M.E.R.C. - Make Every Rep Count Health and Fitness	$14.99		
Mercenary In Love – J.L. Rose & J.L. Turner	$14.99		
Money Make Me Cum – Ernest Morris	$14.99		
My Besties – Asia Hill	$14.99		
My Besties 2 – Asia Hill	$14.99		
My Besties 3 – Asia Hill	$14.99		
My Besties 4 – Asia Hill	$14.99		
My Boyfriend's Wife - Mychea	$14.99		
My Boyfriend's Wife 2 – Mychea	$14.99		
My Brothers Envy – J. L. Rose	$14.99		
My Brothers Envy 2 – J. L. Rose	$14.99		
Naughty Housewives – Ernest Morris	$14.99		
Naughty Housewives 2 – Ernest Morris	$14.99		
Naughty Housewives 3 – Ernest Morris	$14.99		
Naughty Housewives 4 – Ernest Morris	$14.99		
Never Be The Same – Silk White	$14.99		
Shades of Revenge – Assa Raymond Baker	$14.99		

umped – Jason Brent	$14.99		
meone's Gonna Get It – Mychea	$14.99		
anded – Silk White	$14.99		
preme & Justice – Ernest Morris	$14.99		
preme & Justice 2 – Ernest Morris	$14.99		
preme & Justice 3 – Ernest Morris	$14.99		
ars of a Hustler - Silk White	$14.99		
ars of a Hustler 2 - Silk White	$14.99		
ars of a Hustler 3 - Silk White	$14.99		
ars of a Hustler 4- Silk White	$14.99		
ars of a Hustler 5 – Silk White	$14.99		
ars of a Hustler 6 – Silk White	$14.99		
e Last Love Letter – Warren Holloway	$14.99		
e Last Love Letter 2 – Warren Holloway	$14.99		
e Panty Ripper - Reality Way	$14.99		
e Panty Ripper 3 – Reality Way	$14.99		
e Solution – Jay Morrison	$14.99		
e Teflon Queen – Silk White	$14.99		
e Teflon Queen 2 – Silk White	$14.99		
e Teflon Queen 3 – Silk White	$14.99		
e Teflon Queen 4 – Silk White	$14.99		
e Teflon Queen 5 – Silk White	$14.99		
e Teflon Queen 6 - Silk White	$14.99		
e Vacation – Silk White	$14.99		
ed To A Boss - J.L. Rose	$14.99		
ed To A Boss 2 - J.L. Rose	$14.99		
ed To A Boss 3 - J.L. Rose	$14.99		
ed To A Boss 4 - J.L. Rose	$14.99		
ed To A Boss 5 - J.L. Rose	$14.99		
me Is Money - Silk White	$14.99		
morrow's Not Promised – Robert Torres	$14.99		
morrow's Not Promised 2 – Robert Torres	$14.99		
vo Mask One Heart – Jacob Spears and Trayvon Jackson	$14.99		
vo Mask One Heart 2 – Jacob Spears and Trayvon Jackson	$14.99		

Two Mask One Heart 3 – Jacob Spears and Trayvon Jackson	$14.99		
Wrong Place Wrong Time – Silk White	$14.99		
Young Goonz – Reality Way	$14.99		
Subtotal:			
Tax:			
Shipping (Free) U.S. Media Mail:			
Total:			

Make Checks Payable To: Good2Go Publishing, 7311 W Glass Lane, Laveen, AZ 8533

CPSIA information can be obtained
at www.ICGtesting.com
Printed in the USA
LVHW041600100320
649602LV00009B/839